U0017159

專門替中國人寫的
英文基本文法
（修訂版）

李家同、海 柏／著

作者序

我們兩人都有過教初級英文的經驗，我們發現我們中國人寫英文句子時，會犯獨特的錯誤，比方說，我們常將兩個動詞連在一起用，我們也會將動詞用成名詞，我們對過去式和現在式毫無觀念。更加不要說現在完成式了。而天生講英文的人是不可能犯這種錯的。

我們還發現一個有趣的現象，那就是很多文法中的基本規則，一般的文法書上反而沒有提，比方說，第三人稱，單數，現在式，動詞要加s，雖然這是個非常重要的規定，很少文法書上會提到這個規則，即使提到，也在很後面的地方。因為很多句子中都要碰到這種情形，又因為文法書上沒有強調，很多人就永遠犯這個錯誤。

兩個動詞連在一起用，對我們中國人來說，是很正常的事，可是在英文裡，這是犯大忌的。令我們大吃一驚的是，居然絕大多數的英文文法書裡根本找不到這個規則。難怪大家一天到晚犯這種錯誤了。

我們這本英文文法書，是專門為中國人寫的。以下是這本書的一些特徵：

我們一開始就強調一些英文文法的基本規定，這些規定都是我們中國人所不太習慣的。也就是說，我們一開始就告訴了讀者，大家不要犯這種錯誤。

我們馬上就進入動詞，理由很簡單，這是我們中國人最弱的地方。如果我們拖到很晚才討論動詞的規則，極可能為時已晚。讀者已有了一些很壞的習慣，無可救藥矣。根據我們的經驗，絕大多數的錯誤，都與動詞有關。這也難怪，中文裡面，哪有什麼動詞的規則？

我們一再叫大家做中翻英，畢竟我們是初學英文，也沒有和外國人生活在一起的環境，不可能在腦子裡一開始就用英文想。我們一定要先想中文，再想英文，這是初學英文者所無法避免的。如果我們會翻譯很多的中文句子，我們已經很厲害了。也會有成就感。

我們強調改錯，因為初學者一定犯錯。

這本書最適合國中三年級的同學和高中一年級的同學唸，如果感到生字多了一點，老師不妨略過那些有生字的句子。只要基本觀念學會，就可以了。我們已經盡量用了最簡單的字。

最後我們要勸告初學的讀者，你們應該多多做練習，練習做多了，你自然不會犯錯。英文文法並沒有太多邏輯可言，很多規則用慣了，習慣成自然，就大功告成矣。到那時候，你一定會很奇怪，為什麼別人會犯那些荒謬的錯誤了。

如果你做了很多練習，記得很多正確的句子型式，總有一天，你說英文的時候，動詞該加S，你就會加S。該用過去式，就會用過去式。兩個動詞也不會連在一起用，疑問句也會用疑問句的語法。那是多麼美好的一天。

　　希望這一天早日到來！

李家同
海　柏

目次

第一章
英文文法的最基本規則

　　英文和我們中文最大的不同，是在動詞，我們中文的動詞很簡單，沒有所謂的第幾人稱，也沒有複數和單數之分，更沒有過去式或進行式，英文可不同了，凡是用動詞的時候，必須注意很多很多的規則，一旦弄錯了，常常是犯了大錯。

　　在這一章，我要將英文最基本的規則一一列下。這些規則都是我們中國人所常常不注意的。

　　為了不要誤導讀者，凡本書內錯誤的句子前面都有"*"的符號。

規則（1）：兩個動詞是不能連在一起用的

　　在中文，我們常說「我是愛你的」，翻成英文，這就變成了：

　　　*I am love you.

　　滑稽的是，這句英文句子犯了大忌，因為 "*am*" 是動詞，

"*love*" 也是動詞，兩個動詞是不能聯在一起用的。這句話的正確說法是：

I love you.　　或者　　I am in love with you.

我們中國人也會說「我喜歡看電視」，翻成英文，這變成：
　　*I love watch television.
這個句子也犯了同樣的錯。

以下幾個句子都是錯的，因為這些句子中都有兩個動詞連在一起的情形：
　　*I hate eat fish.
　　*I love play basketball.
　　*I love swim.

如果你一定要講「我愛游泳」，怎麼辦呢？請看以下的規則。

 規則(2)：如一定要同時用兩個動詞，後者的前面必須加"to"或者將後者加上"ing"

「我愛游泳」，因此有兩種正確的譯法：
　　1. I love to swim.
　　2. I love swimming.

以下的句子都是正確的：

1. I hate to eat fish.

2. I hate eating fish.

3. I love to play basketball.

4. I love playing basketball

5. I keep going to church.

 ## 規則（3）：主詞如果是第三人稱，現在式及單數，動詞必須加 "s"

我們中國人最不容易記得的規則，恐怕就是這一條了，以下的句子都是錯的。

*He write very well.

*Jack love playing the violin.

*Mary swim every day.

正確的句子是：

1. He writes very well.

2. Jack loves playing the violin.

3. Mary swims every day.

規則（4）：絕大多數的否定句子，不能直接加 "not"

我們中文對否定語氣，規則極為簡單，我們可以說「我不愛你」，但是我們不能說：

*I not love you.

我們也不能說：

*I not saw that movie.

*I not like swimming.

*He not likes playing violin.

我們必須用一種助動詞來完成否定的句子，以下才是正確的否定句子：

1. I do not love you.

2. I did not see that movie.

3. He does not like playing violin.

請注意，在以上的句子中，*do* 和 *did* 都是助動詞，*do* 是現在式，*did* 是過去式。關於現在式和過去式，究竟是怎麼一回事，以後我們會解釋清楚的。

助動詞不限於 *do* 和它的變型，"*can, will, would, shall, may, must*" 等等都是助動詞，因此，以下的英文句子又都是對的：

1. He can not swim.

2. They will not go to church tomorrow.

3. Mary should not go to the party.

4. I shall not see you.

5. He may not go out tonight.

6. He must not eat meat any more.

規則（5）：在不定詞"to"的後面，必須用原形動詞

英文中的動詞，是會變化的，以*have*爲例，第一人稱和第三人就不同：

1. I have a dog.

2. He has a dog.

如果是過去式，動詞又要變化。*have*的過去式是*had*，不論第幾人稱，一概都要用*had*。

幾乎每一個英文動詞的過去式都有變化，以下是幾個例子：

現在式	過去式
go	went
come	came
eat	ate
play	played
swim	swam

不論那一個動詞，都有一個原形動詞，一切都是從這個原

形動詞變出來的，像"*go, drink, have, walk, love, like*"等等都是原形動詞。

如果我們有必要用不定詞"to"，就必須用原形動詞，例如"*to go, to drink, to have*"都是正確的，*to went, *to drank, *to loved等等都是錯的。

英文中有一個動詞最爲麻煩，那就是"*am, are, is, was, were*"等等，翻譯成中文，這都是，而這些動詞的來源都是*be*，所以我們說這些動詞都是be動詞。

以下的句子都用上了"be"

　　1. I want to be a teacher.

　　2. He wants to be a good father.

　　3. They all love to be rich.

　　4. No one likes to be poor.

規則(6)：英文中有所謂的助動詞，必須注意

英文中有很多句子都有助動詞，在規則(4)中，我們說在絕大多數的否定語句中，必須用助動詞*do*或*did*。*do*是原形動詞，*did* 和*does*都是*do*的變形。

除了*do*是助動詞以外，"*can, may, might, will, would, must*"也都是助動詞。

以上所提到的助動詞，都有一個共同的特色，那就是這些助動詞後的動詞必須是原形動詞。

以下的句子都是正確的：

1. He can swim.

2. He does not swim.

3. I do not speak English.

4.You must walk to work every day.

5. I did not work yesterday.

6. You may leave now.

7. I will go to Taipei tomorrow.

以下的句子都是錯的：

＊I did not went.

＊He does not goes to work.

＊You must walked to work.

除了以上的助動詞以外，還有一個非常特殊的助動詞，那就是*have*，在這個助動詞的後面，動詞絕對不能用原形動詞，以下是用這個助動詞的例子：

1. I have been to England.

2. I have slept all day.

3. I have studied English since I was a child.

*been, slept*和*studied*都是過去分詞（past participle），以下的句子也都是現在完成式，我們以後討論完成式的時候，會將這些解釋清楚的。

規則(7)：英文問句要有助動詞

我們先看看以下的英文句子，這些都是錯的：

*Why you drink so much water?

*How many books you wrote?

*How many sons you have?

正確的句子是：

Why do you drink so much water?

How many books did you write?

How many sons do you have?

絕大多數的英文問句子是一定要有助動詞，以下全是正確的英文問句，你可以看出每一句的助動詞嗎？

1. Do you love me?

2. Did you go to school yesterday?

3. How many books do you have?

4. How much money does he have?

5. Why don't you go back home?

6. Do you like to swim?

7. Can you play violin?

8. Will you go home tomorrow?

9. Would you give me a call?

　　當然啦，一旦動詞是 *verb to be*，我們又不需要助動詞了，以下都是正確的英文問句：

1. Are you a teacher?

2. Is he a student?

3. Is Mr. Chang your father?

4. Were your mother and father in England last year?

 規則（8）：特殊動詞隨主詞的變化

　　英文中，有些動詞因主詞不同而改變，*verb to be* 是其中之一，因此，我們必須記得以下的規則：

		第一人稱	第二人稱	第三人稱
現在式	單數	I am	You are	(He, She, It)is
	複數	We are	You are	They are
過去式	單數	I was	You were	(He, She, It)was
	複數	We were	You were	They were

Verb to have也有類似的變化：

		第一人稱	第二人稱	第三人稱
現在式	單數	I have	You have	(He, She, It)has
	複數	We have	You have	They have
過去式	單數	I had	You had	(He, She, It)had
	複數	We had	You had	They had

練習一

以下的句子都有錯，請將正確的句子寫出來：

1. I am love my parents.

2. He is loves his teacher.

3. He keeps swim every day.

4. He wants drink a glass of water.

5. He likes play the violin.

6. Jack do not like mathematics.

7. Mary hate singing.

8. My mother cook very good food.

9. He want me to see him tomorrow.

10. He not knows my name.

11. I not like you.

12. He not like swimming.

13. You not went home.

14. I not like swimming.

15. I wanted to went to my mother's home.

16. I do not like to swimming.

17. I did not ate dinner.

18. I will not went home.

19. He did not went home.

20. You may leaving now.

21. He can swimming.

22. He does not goes to work.

第二章
現在式和現在進行式

![筆筒] 2.1 現在式

英文中，現在式(present tense)好像是最容易的，其實現在式是我們常常用錯的時式。

首先，我們不妨舉一個例子來說明我們對現在式慣有的誤解，假設我們要說「我在吃午飯」，這總該用現在式了吧。很多人將這句話翻成：*I eat lunch.

這就錯了，因為「*I eat lunch.*」的意思並不是「我在吃午飯」，而是「我有吃午飯的習慣」，意思是說，「有人中午不吃午飯(可能是在減肥)，可是我每天中午都會吃午飯的」。

「我在吃午飯」，應該要用現在進行式，這是我們以後會談的。

現在式不是指任何一個行為，而是一種狀況。舉例來說，以下幾句話都應該用現在式：

1.我是一個學生。　　　　　I am a student.

2.他是一個老師。　　　　　He is a teacher.

3.他每天游泳。　　　　　　He swims every day.

4.湯姆勤奮工作。　　　　　Tom works hard.

5.他早起。　　　　　　　　He gets up early.

6.瑪莉喜歡看電影。　　　　Mary loves watching movies.

7.這裡常常下雨。　　　　　It rains often here.

8.他們都很懶。　　　　　　They are all very lazy.

9.我是中國人。　　　　　　I am a Chinese.

10.他會講英文。　　　　　　He speaks English.

11.他有喝茶的習慣。　　　　He drinks tea.

12.我騎腳踏車上學。　　　　I ride a bicycle to school.

13.他搭乘公車上班。　　　　He rides a bus to go to work.

14.我不喜歡你。　　　　　　I do not like you.

15.他愛他的太太。 He loves his wife.

16.他守法。 He obeys the law.

17.我不喜歡莎士比亞。 I do not like Shakespeare.

18.他不抽煙。 He does not smoke.

19.他喝酒。 He drinks.

20.他唱歌唱得很好。 He sings well.

21.他跳舞跳得很好。 He dances well.

22.他不會游泳。 He can not swim.

23.他不是一個好學生。 He is not a good student.

24.我每天喝一杯牛奶。 I drink a glass of milk every day.

凡是真理，自然界的現象，數學裡的定理，都要用現在式：

1.太陽從東方升起。 The sun rises in the east.

2.地球是圓的。 The earth is round.

3.月亮是地球的一個衛星。 The moon is a satellite of the earth.

4.美國是一個大的國家。　　　　America is a large country.

5.在北極的夏天，太陽永不落下。　The sun never sets at the North Pole in summer.

6.樹葉吸收二氧化碳。　　　　　　Tree leaves absorb CO_2.

7.電腦的基本原理是布林代數。　The basic principle of computers is Boolean algebra.

8.二點決定一線。　　　　　　Two points define a line.

9.三點決定一平面。　　　　　Three points define a plane.

10.三基本顏色是紅、黃、藍。　The three basic colors are red, yellow and blue.

練習二

將以下中文句子翻成英文，都用現在式。

1.他是一個好學生。

2.我的哥哥17歲。

3.我弟弟每天游泳。

4.他們都喜歡音樂。

5.他們現在在日本。

6.玉山是很高的山。

7.亞馬遜河是很長的河。

8.他的爸爸是位老師。

9.我們都喜歡中國菜。

10.他不喜歡冰淇淋。

11.我愛你。

12.每個人都怕蛇。

13.每個人都喜歡狗。

14.今天真冷。

2.2 現在進行式

假如我們正在做一件事，是不能用現在式的，而必須用現在進行式，現在進行式的形態是：

verb to be + present participle（現在分詞）

verb to be 大家都懂，什麼叫做現在分詞呢？現在分詞就是：動詞＋*ing*

以下是現在分詞的例子：

動詞	現在分詞
work	working
go	going
read	reading
run	running
play	playing
swim	swimming
sing	singing
write	writing
eat	eating
walk	walking
come	coming
love	loving
like	liking
watch	watching
smoke	smoking

如果我們說：

I am watching a movie.

那是指我現在正在看電影，這和：

I watch movies.

意義上截然不同的，I watch movies是說我有看電影的習慣。

因此有些動詞是沒有現在進行式的，舉例來說：

*I am loving you.

是不通的，因為嚴格說起來，*love*是一種狀態，而不是一個動作。現在進行式，都是指動作，很少指狀態的。以下是現在進行式的例子：

1. I am calling my father.

2. He is swimming now.

3. He is playing basketball.

4. They are all eating now.

5. He is walking in the woods now.

6. He is reading a detective novel.

7. Mr. Brown is driving to work.

8. Mrs. Brown is cooking.

9. It is raining now.

練習三

將以下句子譯成英文，都用現在進行式：

1.他在看電影。

2.我在游泳。

3.她在和她媽媽打電話。

4.他的哥哥在散步。

5.我現在正在吃飯。

6.我們在唱歌。

7.他在彈鋼琴。

8.他在看一本小說。

9.我在寫一封信。

10.他在跑步。

練習四

將下列句子譯成英文，有的用現在式，有的用現在進行式：

1.我愛你。

2.我正在吃飯。

3.他不是一個學生。

4.我是一個老師。

5.我正在唱歌。

6.他在游泳。

7.他喜歡游泳。

8.他會唱歌。

9.他正在唱歌。

10.他的爸爸是一個醫生。

11.他的爸爸在美國。

12.我正在洗澡。

13.他正在睡覺。

14.你的姊姊在騎腳踏車。

15.你的姊姊每天騎腳踏車上學。

第三章

過去式和過去進行式

3.1 過去式

過去式是指過去所發生的事，舉例來說，假如我昨天去看了一場電影，我就可以說：

I went to see a movie yesterday.

以下全部是正確的句子：

1. I saw your father last night.

2. I met your son last month.

3. I ate three apples this morning.

4. He went to church to pray last night.

可是，我們必須非常小心，因為一不小心，我們就可能犯了大錯，我們如果要向情侶表示愛情，當然說：I love you.

如果我們說：

I loved you.

事情就可能鬧大了，因為這表示我過去曾經愛過你，可是現在已經不愛了："I loved you"等於是"I loved you before. But I do not love you now."

假如我們看過一個小男孩然後我們說：

He was a good boy.

那就是說他現在已不是一個好男孩了，變成了一個不乖的孩子，或者他已經死了。

英文裡的過去式常常是偵探用來破案的線索。有一次，有一個母親，向警察報案，說她的女兒失蹤了，她在記者面前，聲淚俱下地說：

She was such a nice girl.

警察馬上覺得這位母親有問題，因為她不該用過去式的，用了過去式，表示女兒已經死了，可是母親不是說她失蹤了嗎？為什麼她用過去式，極有可能因為她知道她女兒已經死了，才脫口而出，用了過去式。警察因此懷疑母親本人就是兇手，事實也果真如此：這位母親打自己的女兒，出手太重，將女兒打死了，謊報女兒失蹤，她用了過去式，使警察知道她有問題。整個案子的偵破，就在於過去式。

我們因此不能輕易用過去式，但我們也千萬要注意，該用過去式的時候，一定要用過去式，以下句子都是錯的：

*I go to school yesterday.

*I see a movie last night.

*My mother comes to see me last month.

*I eat three apples this morning.

*He is happy yesterday.

以上句子的正確寫法是：

1. I went to school yesterday.

2. I saw a movie last night.

3. My mother came to see me last month.

4. I ate three apples this morning.

5. He was happy yesterday.

練習五

將以下中文句子翻成英文，全部用過去式：

1.我昨天參加了一個舞會。

2.他的哥哥昨天打電話給我。

3.我去年到美國去。

4.昨夜我遇到你的姊姊。

5.我寫了一封信給你。

6.我今晨吃了一個蛋。

7.他昨夜整夜跳舞。

8.我們昨天跑了五千公尺。

9.他昨夜非常疲倦。

10.他昨夜去台北探訪他的爸爸。

練習六

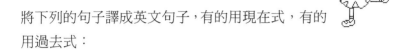

將下列的句子譯成英文句子,有的用現在式,有的用過去式:

1.他是一個強壯的男孩。

2.他昨天生病了。

3.他每天吃一個蘋果。

4.他昨天吃了三個蘋果。

5.我喜歡看電影。

6.我是個快樂的人。

7.昨天我看了兩場電影。

8.他昨天寄了一封信給你。

9.他常常抽煙。

10.我每天讀聖經。

11.他昨天沒有唸聖經。

12.他昨天沒有游泳。

練習七

將以下句子譯成英文，用現在式，現在進行式或過去式：

1.他在打籃球。

2.他喜歡打籃球。

3.他昨天打籃球。

4.他每天騎腳踏車上學。

5.他昨天騎腳踏車到鄉下去。

6.我喜歡唱歌。

7.他正在唱歌。

8.你的爸爸昨天來看我。

9.他的哥哥每天步行二公里。

10.他的弟弟是個好孩子。

11.他去年非常虛弱。

12.他正在打電話。

13.他每天都努力工作(work hard)。

14.你的弟弟喜歡游泳。

15.他過去是個好學生。

3.2 過去進行式

過去進行式和現在進行式有點類似，只是 *verb to be* 要用過去式的。可是有一點不同，過去進行式，很少單獨用的，而常和另一句子一齊用。舉例來說以下的中文句子：

我昨天去看你的時候，你正在打籃球，如譯成英文，就是：

> You were playing basketball when I went to see you yesterday.

以下是典型的過去進行式用法：

1. I was taking a bath when you called.
2. I was watching TV when you came to see me.
3. They were dancing when the teacher came in.
4. They were singing in the station when the train arrived.
5. Mr. Brown was cleaning his house when his son came home.

總而言之，過去進行式通常牽涉到幾件事，這兩件事同時發生，其中一件事用過去式，另一件事用過去進行式。

練習八

將以下句子譯成英文，其中一部份使用過去進行式：

1.他昨天到學校去的時候，天在下雨。

2.當火車停下的時候，他在看報（read newspaper）。

3.當火車進站的時候，他們在唱歌。

4.我昨天去他家的時候，他在和他爸爸打電話。

5.昨天晚上八點鐘，我在家看電視。

6.當我爸爸昨晚打電話給我的時候，我正在刷牙（brush my teeth）。

7.當我昨晚打電話給他時，他在游泳。

8.當這貓走進來的時候，那隻狗在睡覺。

9.當他弟弟回家的時候，他在拉小提琴。

10.當我爸爸回家的時候，我媽媽在燒飯。

練習九

填充：

1. I _____（be）a Christian.

2. He _____（be）a Catholic when he was a child.

3. I _____（go）to see my mother yesterday.

4. I _____（like）to play the piano.

5. He _____（eat）now.

6. He _____（like）to eat ice cream.

7. He _____（walk）to school every day.

8. He _____（walk）now.

9. He _____（be）a good boy.

10. He _____（swim）when I called him.

11. He _____ (go) to see his mother yesterday.

12. I _____ (take) a bath when my mother called me.

13. I _____ (like) to swim.

14. I _____ (like) to swim when I was young.　Now, I don't

because I am too old.

15. It _____ (rain) now.

16. It _____ (rain) when I drove to work yesterday.

17. It _____ (rain) last night.

18. It _____ (rain) very　often　here.

19. He _____ (read) a book when I went to see him yesterday.

20. I _____ (be) a student when I was young. Now I am a

teacher.

練習十

改正以下句子的錯誤：

1. They are driving when I went to see them yesterday.

2. It rained very often in Taipei.

3. He gives his book to his brother last month.

4. He go to work every morning.

5. He likes to told stories.

6. I like to went to church.

7. The sun sets now.

8. They are play the piano now.

9. I am love you.

10. He were a good student before.

11. He goes to church last Sunday.

12. It rains last night.

13. I am playing when you called.

14. It is raining when I drove to work last night.

15. He do not know me.

16. I were swimming when my mother came.

17. They is singing now.

18. He do not like to swim.

19. He always wear a black coat.

20. He is watch TV now.

第四章

完成式

4.1 現在完成式（Present Perfect Tense）

完成式的形式是 *verb to have + past participle*，每一個動詞，都有過去式和過去分詞，以下就是一些例子：

（1）規則動詞

這些動詞的過去式和過去分詞，都只要加"ed"

原式	過去式	過去分詞（past participle）
arrive	arrived	arrived
dance	danced	danced
kill	killed	killed
listen	listened	listened
love	loved	loved
paint	painted	painted

原式	過去式	過去分詞（past participle）
snow	snowed	snowed
use	used	used
walk	walked	walked
watch	watched	watched
work	worked	worked

（2）不規則動詞

這些動詞的過去式和過去分詞，沒有一定的規則

原式	過去式	過去分詞（past participle
break	broke	broken
buy	bought	bought
come	came	come
do	did	done
draw	drew	drawn
eat	ate	eaten
fly	flew	flown
get	got	gotten
go	went	gone
grow	grew	grown
have	had	had
hit	hit	hit
leave	left	left
read	read	read
ride	rode	ridden
run	ran	run
see	saw	seen
sell	sold	sold
sing	sang	sung
spread	spread	spread

原式	過去式	過去分詞（past participle）
steal	stole	stolen
swim	swam	swum
take	took	taken
write	wrote	written

以下的句子都用了現在完成式：

1. I have read this book.

2. I have seen the movie.

3. I have lived here since 1973.

4. I have studied English for a long time.

5. He has washed his hands.

6. He has left.

7. He has already completed the report.

8. The storm has arrived.

9. I have taken the job.

10. I have written the letters.

11. I have not seen him since 1975.

12. I have never seen this man before.

那麼，在什麼情況之下要用現在完成式呢？

(1)首先假設我們有一件事，發生在過去，而一直延續到現在，就要用現在完成式，這種句子後面常有"*since*"或"*for*"。以下是這種情形的例子：

1. 自從1963年，我一直在唸英文。

   I have studied English since 1963.

2. 自從1975年以後，我就住在這裡。

   I have lived here since 1975.

3. 自從我是一個小孩子，我就喜歡搖滾樂。

   I have loved rock and roll music since I was a child.

4. 自從去年，我就從來沒有見過他。

   Since last year, I have never seen him.

5. 自從1950年以後，他就一直在此工作。

   He has worked here since 1950.

6. 我認識他已經很久了。

   I have known him for a long time.

7. 他練習網球已經四年了。

   He has already practiced tennis for (the past) four years.

8. 我穿這件夾克很久了。

   I have worn this jacket for a very long time.

9. 我開這輛汽車很久了。

   I have driven this car for a long time.

10. 好久沒有下雨了。

    It has not rained for a long time.

(2)使用現在完成式的另一情況是強調已經完成的事，比方說，
你說「我已經寫了那封信」，就可以用現在完成式，或者，
你說「他已經完成了工作」。以下是這類的例子：

1.我已經寫了這封信。

I have already written the letter.

2.他已經完成了工作。

He has already completed the work.

3.我已經測試了這個程式。

I have already tested the program.

4.我已經收到了你的信。

I have already received your letter.

5.他已搬到了一個較大的房子。

He has already moved to a bigger house.

6.雖然他很年輕，但他已寫了三本小說。

Although he is young, he has already written three novels.

7.我打了二次電話給他，他都沒有回答。

I called him twice. He has never answered.

(3)現在完成式用來表示一種經驗，舉例來說，「我曾經到過美
國」、「我曾見過李總統」、「我有生以來沒有跳過舞」，
這些都應該用現在完成式，例如：

1.我曾經到過美國。

I have been to America.

2.我曾見過李總統。

I have seen President Lee.

3.我有生以來沒有跳過舞。

I have never danced in my life.

4.我看過「雙城記」。

I have read *The Tale of Two Cities*.

5.他曾吃過這種冰淇淋。

He has tasted this kind of ice cream.

6.我未曾見過雪。

I have never seen snow.

7.你曾見過雪嗎？

Have you ever seen snow?

8.你登過玉山嗎？

Have you ever climbed Jade Mountain？

(4)現在完成式可以用來表示一件過去常發生的事

1.今年我國已有二次颱風。

We have already had two typhoons so far this year.

2.他今年已發表了三篇論文。

He has already published three papers this year.

3.過去一年,我看了三次「鐵達尼號」。

In the past year, I have seen the movie *Titanic* three times.

　　對讀者而言,最重要的是現在完成式和過去式不同究竟在那裡?最重要的不同在於,一旦在句子中講一件過去發生的事,而且指定特定的時間,就一定要用過去式,而不能用現在完成式。比方說,「我曾經看過『鐵達尼號』」,可以用現在完成式,因為這句話沒有指明任何特定的時間,假如說,「我昨天晚上去看『鐵達尼號』」,就一定用過去式,讀者不妨看看以下的比較:

　　　　a. I went to America last year.

　　　　　I have been to America.

　　　　b. I saw the movie *Titanic* last year.

　　　　　I have seen the movie *Titanic* twice.

　　　　c. I finished my homework late last night.

　　　　　I have finally finished my homework.

　　　　d. I studied English when I was a small child.

　　　　　I have studied English since I was a child.

e. I went to church yesterday.

I have never been to church.

以下的句子是錯的，請特別注意：

＊I have seen the movie last year.

＊I have never been to America last year.

＊He has never finished his work last night.

現在完成式常和 *since, for, already, never, ever* 等字一起使用，以下都是這類的例子：

1. I have already had dinner.

2. Since this summer began, we have already had two storms.

3. It has not rained for a long time.

4. I have never talked to this man before.

5. I have never met your father.

6. Have you ever been to America?

7. He has already won three awards.

8. I have stayed here since June.

Never 和 *ever* 也常是我們弄不清楚如何使用的字，一般說來，*never* 有否定的意思，*ever* 則只有在問句中才會出現。

練習十一

將以下句子譯成英文，全部用現在完成式：

1.自從1980年，我就每天早上游泳。

2.我已收到了你的信。

3.我從未去過美國。

4.從他是一個小孩開始，他就是一個基督徒（Christian）。

5.我見過你的祖父。

6.你的弟弟一直住在這裡。

7.他學鋼琴已經很久了。

8.我已寫了三封信給他，他都沒有回。

9.過去三年我都在開這部車。

10.自從1975年以來，他一直是一位老師。

11.他教英文很久了。

12.我曾經看過「亂世佳人」(*Gone with the Wind*)。

13.我已吃過飯了。

14.今年我去過海灘三次。

15.我終其一生都愛你的。

練習十二

將以下句子譯成英文，有的用過去式，有的用現在完成式：

1.昨天我去看「亂世佳人」（*Gone with the Wind*）。

2.我從未看過「亂世佳人」（*Gone with the Wind*）。

3.去年，我住在美國。

4.自從1985年，我就一直住在美國。

5.他從未去過英國。

6.他已經完成了報告。

7.我昨天晚上完成了報告。

8.昨夜，我見到了你的父親。

9.我已經見過你的父親好幾次了。

10.我終生都住在台中。

練習十三

填充：

1. I _____ (become) a Christian already since I was a child.

2. I _____ (be) a Christian all my life.

3. He _____ (live) here since 1939.

4. Stop eating now. You _____ (eat) too much.

5. It _____ (rain) last night.

6. John is a writer. He _____ (write) thirteen novels.

7. Last night, I _____(see) your father for the first time in my life.

8. I _____ (talk) to my father last night.

9. Since 1961, I _____ (be) a teacher. Before that, I _____ (be) a student.

10. I _____ (read) many novels written by Charles Dickens.

4.2 現在完成進行式 (Present Perfect Progressive Tense)

在上一節，我們知道，如果有一個行動，從過去發生後，就一直延續到現在，我們可以用現在完成式。舉例來說，以下的例子都應該用現在完成式：

1.自從1974年，我就在學校學英文。

Since 1974, I have studied English at school.

2.自從我大學畢業以後，我就在這裡工作。

Since I graduated from college, I have worked here.

以第一句話為例，假如我們要強調我一直在學英文，而且沒有間斷，我們可以用現在完成進行式（present perfect progressive tense）。所謂現在完成進行式，形式如下：

verb to have + been + present participle

verb to have　是為了完成式，been 和 present participle 都是為了進行式。

以下是現在完成進行式的例子：

1. I have been studying English since 1974.

2. I have been working here since I graduated from college.

3. I have been living here since I was a child.

4. He has been acting like a fool lately. (他最近一直在做傻事)

5. They have been dancing since seven o'clock.

6. It has been snowing since yesterday.

7. I have been taking music lessons since last year.

8. He has been drinking heavily since last year. (他去年起，就一直在酗酒)

練習十四

將以下的句子譯成英文，全部用現在完成進行式：

1.自從我們是小孩子起，我們就一直努力工作。

2. 從去年起，他就在唸英文。

3. 從昨天起，就一直在下雨。

4. 從五時起，他就在做功課(do homework)。

5. 從三歲起，我就一直住在台中。

4.3 過去完成式和過去完成進行式 (Past Perfect Tense and Past Perfect Progressive Tense)

過去完成式的形式如下:

had + past participle

過去完成式是不能單獨用的。我們用的時候,必須有另一個事件。也就是說,假如我們有兩件事A和B,兩件事都發生在過去,但A發生在B以前,A應該用過去完成式,B則用過去式。以下是幾個例子:

1. 他到台灣以前,曾學過中文。

   He had studied Chinese before he came to Taiwan.

2. 他唸大學以前,曾經工作過。

   He had worked before he decided to go to college.

3. 我寫這篇有關愛爾蘭的小說以前,曾去過愛爾蘭。

   I had been to Ireland before I wrote this novel about Ireland.

4. 我在上大學以前,已經學過微積分。

   I had studied calculus before I got into college.

5.週一以前，已經下過雪了。

It had already snowed before Monday.

如果我們要強調較早發生事件的連續性，我們可以用過去完成進行式。過去完成進行式和現在完成進行式唯一不同的地方是 *verb to have* 的地方一定要用 *had* 。以下是一些過去完成進行式的例子：

1. I had been watching TV before you called me.

2. I had been working hard in a company for many years before I went to college.

3. He had been studying before he went to class.

4. He had been driving all day before he went to sleep.

練習十五

將以下中文句子譯成英文，請注意何處該用過去式，何處該用過去完成式或過去完成進行式：

1.我十四歲以前，就曾見過你的母親。

2.我1974年以前，曾去過美國。

3.六年前，他唸過聖經(the Bible)。

4.我唸大學以前，曾經是個工程師(engineer)。

5.你來以前，我曾打電話給你。

6.在我昨天晚上和李先生吃飯以前，曾和他見過面。

7.在他辭職(resign)以前，他是個好校長(president)。

8.在他去世(die)前，他是個好醫生。

9.在他到教堂以前，他一直在練習唱歌。

10.在今天早上八時以前，天一直在下雨。

練習十六

將以下的中文句子譯成英文，選適宜的時態。

1.他昨天去看你的時候，你在唱歌。

2.他從前是個好孩子。

3.他們都喜歡打籃球。

4.我們正在看電視。

5.你在台灣住了很久了。

6.我已經看完了這本書。

7.他們一直都住在這裡。

8.我來以前，曾去過教堂。

9.他喜歡看日出。

10.他喜歡游泳。

11.他自從六歲起，就一直在學鋼琴(piano)。

12.他過去是個強壯的孩子。

13.在他生病以前，他曾是個非常健康(healthy)的人。

14.當火車進站時，人們在跳舞。

15.在戰爭爆發(break out)以前，他曾是個音樂家(musician)。

16.我曾見過你。

17.我去年見過你。

18.我已經將信寫好了。

19.自從1974年以來，我就是一個軍人(soldier)。

20.我讀了很多英文書。

練習十七

將正確的動詞填入以下各句的空白（有的地方可能有多種答案）

1. He _____ (love) his country.

2. He _____ (love) his country, but now he does not.

3. I _____ (be) a teacher since 1975.

4. I _____ (be) a teacher before I went to college.

5. I _____ (read) Shakespeare ever since I was a little girl.

6. When I went to see her yesterday, she _____ (watch) TV.

7. I _____ (see) your father before I saw you.

8. He _____ (read) many detective stories.

9. He _____ (go) to church every Sunday.

10. It _____ (be) a cold day yesterday.

11. It _____ (rain) for the last two days.

12. I _____ (eat) too much.　I am full now.

13. She _____ (be) a nurse before the war broke out.

14. I _____ (have) never _____ (see) you in my life.

15. He _____ (be) a teacher since 1980.

16. It _____ (be) good to eat vegetables every day.

17. It _____ (be) so nice to meet you last night.

18. She _____ (be) such a nice girl before she died.

19. Peter _____ (go) to America many times.

20. He _____ (work) hard since last year. He _____
    (hope) to succeed in the college entrance examination this
    time.

第五章
未來式

5.1 未來式的基本規則

　　如果我們在句子中，有需要提到未來的事情，就可以使用未來式，舉例來說，以下的句子都用未來式。

　　　1. I will go to America tomorrow.

　　　2. He will dance tonight.

　　　3. Peter will finish his work next month.

　　如果不用"*will*"，我們可以用"*verb to be +going to+ verb*"，如果我們如此做，以上的三個句子就變成了以下的句子：

　　　1. I am going to go to America tomorrow.

　　　2. He is going to dance tonight.

　　　3. Peter is going to finish his work next month.

以下是一些未來式的例子：

1. I will call you tonight.

   I am going to call you tonight.

2. He will graduate next June.

   He is going to graduate next June.

3. Mr. Lee will teach us English soon.

   Mr. Lee is going to teach us English soon.

4. He will help you.

   He is going to help you.

5. The war will break out soon.

   The war is going to break out soon.

6. It will rain tonight.

   It is going to rain tonight.

有一個規則必須注意，就是"*will*"是一個助動詞，現在式第三人稱單數的主詞，仍不用在"*will*"後面加"s"。

不僅如此，"*will*"後面的動詞必須用成原式，如果用 "*verb to be+going to+verb*"這裡面的"*verb*"也必須用原式。因為這裡面的"*to*"是"*infinitive*"，"*infinitive*"後面永遠要用原型動詞。

以下的例子都是錯的：

*He wills go to school.

*He will goes to school.

*They will went to work tomorrow.

*Tom is going to saw me tonight.

*Peter is going to working next month.

未來式常和別的句子用在一起，以下是典型的例子：

1. When you come tomorrow, I will already be in Taipei.

2. After I graduate, I am going to be a good doctor in Africa.

3. Before I leave tomorrow, I will finish my work.

4. After the war is over, every one will be happy.

5. I will go to a concert after my classes are over.

6. I will eat lunch as soon as I have time.

但千萬不可寫出以下錯誤的句子：

*When you will come tomorrow, I will already be in Taipei.

*After the war will be over, every one will be happy.

*I will eat lunch as soon as I will have time.

練習十八

將以下的中文句子翻成英文句子,用"will"或"to be going to":

1.我明天要上教堂(go to church)。

2.他下週一要和我見面。

3.他明天要整理這間房間(clean this room)。

4.我明天吃晚飯後要去台北。

5.我明天晚上回家以後,就打電話給你。

6.我畢業以後會去唸法律。

7.明天你走以後,我要看電視. 。

8.明天我會去台南。

9.今天晚上我要寫一封信給你。

10.今晚,我要等我的哥哥。

練習十九

填充：

1. I _____ (be) in America next year after I _____
   (graduate).

2. I _____ (explain) this to you tonight after I _____
   (read) the report.

3. I _____ (see) you tonight.

4. As soon as you _____ (come) to see me, I _____ (give)
   you my book.

5. When you _____ (arrive) in New York tomorrow, Tom __
   (be) in the airport to meet you.

6. I _____ (go) to church after the rain stops.

7. I _____ (watch) the new TV program after you _____
   (leave).

8. When you _____ (get) here tomorrow, everyone _____
   (wait) for you.

9. I _____ (get) a job as soon as I get out of college.

10. He_____ (have) dinner very late tomorrow.

11. I_____ (quit) my present job, after I_____ (find) a
    better one.

5.2 未來式的變形

未來式可以和進行式合起來用，以下是未來進行式的例子：

1. I will be watching TV tomorrow at eight.
2. He will be eating a big dinner after he gets out of the hospital.
3. I will be studying mathematics at home when you come.
4. Two days later, I will be driving a new car.

未來式可以和完成式合在一起用，而成為未來完成式，這種句子都是在於強調未來要完成的事。舉例來說，「我明天六點以前，我會完成這工作了」，就可以用未來完成式：

I will have finished this work by six o'clock tomorrow.

以下是一些未來完成式的例子：

1. By the time he arrives at the station, the train will have left.
2. We will have had three meetings before six o'clock tonight.
3. He will have written six novels next summer.

練習二十

填充（用未來進行式或未來完成式）：

1. I _____ （watch）the baseball game tomorrow night.

2. He _____（finish）the report when you arrive at his home.

3. I _____ （wash）my car tonight when my mother comes.

4. They _____ （play）their violins when the clock strikes twelve.

5. He _____ （complete）writing this program before ten o'clock tonight.

6. He _____ （be）the president for three years next May.

7. I _____ （repair）my car when you come tonight.

8. I _____ （read）this report before six o'clock tomorrow evening.

9. People _____ （dance）in the streets if Mr. Robertson is elected president.

10. I _____ （drive）four hundred miles tomorrow.

練習二十一

將以下中文句子譯成英文：

1. 彼得生於1965年，他從小就喜歡音樂，自從1975年起，他就一直在練習小提琴。現在他是一個很好的小提琴家。

2. 我的哥哥明天會來看我，他來的時候，我會在家裡看電視。我喜歡看有關醫院的節目。

3. 在我小的時候我常常喜歡打籃球，現在我不打籃球了，因為我曾有一次車禍(car accident)。

4. 我現在在打電話給我的母親，我的母親現在88歲，他在台北已經住了60年。

5. 在我去美國以前，我曾經去過英國，當我在英國的時候，我碰見了一個美麗的女孩子，他後來成為我的太太。

練習二十二

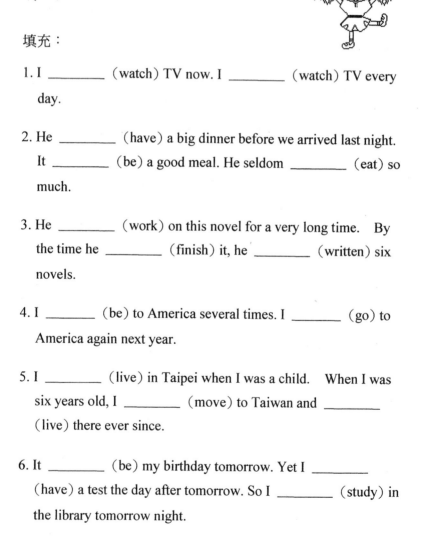

填充：

1. I _____ (watch) TV now. I _____ (watch) TV every
day.

2. He _____ (have) a big dinner before we arrived last night.
It _____ (be) a good meal. He seldom _____ (eat) so
much.

3. He _____ (work) on this novel for a very long time.   By
the time he _____ (finish) it, he _____ (written) six
novels.

4. I _____ (be) to America several times. I _____ (go) to
America again next year.

5. I _____ (live) in Taipei when I was a child.   When I was
six years old, I _____ (move) to Taiwan and _____
(live) there ever since.

6. It _____ (be) my birthday tomorrow. Yet I _____
(have) a test the day after tomorrow. So I _____ (study) in
the library tomorrow night.

7. He _____ (be) a strong kid before he became an athlete in college. Now although he _____ (be) seventy years old, he _____ (be) still quite healthy.

8. He _____ (take) a bath every morning. Today, since he _____ (get) up very late, he _____ (go) to school directly without taking a bath.

第六章

否定句

6.1 否定句的基本規則

在任何語言，我們都有必要造出「否定」的句子，在中文，寫出否定句子並非難事，在英文，無論任何否定句子，都必須遵行一些規定，以下是否定句子的例子：

肯定句	否定句
I like music.	I don't like music.
He loves swimming.	He does not love swimming.
They have come to work.	They have not come to work.
Mary went to see a movie yesterday.	Mary did not go to see a movie yesterday.
John is a good boy.	John is not a good boy.

肯定句	否定句
I will go to New York tomorrow.	I will not go to New York tomorrow.
He can sing.	He can not sing.
You may go now.	You may not go now.
He should sleep early.	He should not sleep early.
It is raining now.	It is not raining now.
It rains very often here.	It does not rain very often here.
He has a lot of money.	He does not have a lot of money.
It is exciting to see this game.	It is not exciting to see this game.
He asked me three questions.	He did not ask me three questions.

從以上的例子來看，我們可以歸納出以下的規則：

1. *"Verb to be"* 後面可以直接加*"not"*

例如：

1. He is not a good teacher.

2. Mary was not very happy when she was young.

3. They are not strong boys.

4. Peter is not coming.

5. John is not going to work.

2. 助動詞後面可以直接加"*not*"

例如：

    1. He has not written any letter.

    2. They will not come.

    3. He cannot swim.

    4. They should not cry very often.

    5. Tom had not eaten any thing before you came.

    6. He may never eat cakes in the future.

    7. John has not lived here.

3. 一般句子的動詞必須加入"*do*"或他的變形

    1. He does not smoke.

    2. He did not go.

    3. I do not love sports.

    4. You do not like to eat fish.

    5. They do not swim very well.

    6. We did not see that movie.

    在英文中，我們可以用"*have to*"來代替"*must*"，以下是"*have to*"的例子：

    1. He has to go to Chicago tomorrow.

      （他明天應該去芝加哥。）

2.They had to buy three tickets to go to the concert.

（他們必須買三張票去聽音樂會。）

3. I have to work very hard.（我必須努力工作。）

含有"*have to*"的句子，如要改成否定句子，必須在 "*have to*" 前面加"*do*"或它的變形，請看以下的例子：

肯定句	否定句
He has to eat a lot of food.	He does not have to eat a lot of food.
He had to leave.	He did not have to leave.
I have to write that letter.	I do not have to write that letter.

練習二十三

將以下的肯定句改成否定句：

1. I saw your brother last night.

2. I like apples.

3. She is a beautiful girl.

4. They can play violin very well.

5. Mr. Chang must answer the following questions.

6. He went to see his brother last night.

7. He could sing many songs.

8. He will buy this car.

9. It rained heavily last night.

10. I have lived here for three years.

11. He has to see his mother.

12. He had to stay here yesterday.

6.2 No, Never和Any的用法

要達成否定的意思,有時我們也可以用"*no*"和"*never*"這些字,"*no*"必須跟一個名詞,請看下面的例子:

1. I saw no students here.

2. There are no lakes in this country.

3. I have no money.

4. I had no choice.

5. He has no friends.

以上這些例子也可以用"*not*"來表示否定的意思,如果用"*not*",則以上的句子應該照下面的方式寫;

1. I did not see any students here.

2. We can not find any lakes in this country.

3. I do not have any money.

4. I did not have any choices.

5. He does not have any friends.

除以上"*not*"之外,"*never*"也可以表達否定的意思,以下都是"*never*"的例子,請注意"*never*"常用在完成式的句子裡:

1. I have never gone there.

2. He has never written any songs.

3. They have never washed their clothes.

練習二十四

用"no"，"not"和"never"填空在以下的句子裡：

1. I have _____ money.

2. A selfish person does _____ have any friends.

3. _____ man is entirely alone.

4. _____ one is living here. We can _____ get into this house.

5. _____ a single person loves me.

6. _____ one loves me.

7. The person whom I saw did _____ come.

8. I did _____ go to work yesterday.

9. I had _____ work to do yesterday.

10. I can _____ find any one in this hall.

11. I have _____ gone to America.

12. He has _____ written to me.

第七章

問句

7.1 答案只是Yes或No的問題

有些問題，答案只有"Yes"或"No"，以下是一些例子：

原來句子	問句
I am a boy.	Am I a boy?
He has a car.	Does he have a car?
I gave him three books.	Did I give him three books?
He cannot work.	Can he work?
He has not seen me.	Has he seen me?
They like your novel.	Do they like your novel?
The sun sets in the west.	Does the sun set in the west?
They are good teachers.	Are they good teachers?

原來句子	問句
He will not go to a concert tonight.	Will he go to a concert tonight?
He is going to swim.	Is he going to swim?
They must eat vegetables.	Must they eat vegetables?
They have to go.	Do they have to go?
I walked two kilometers yesterday.	Did I walk two kilometers yesterday?
It is raining now.	Is it raining now?

根據以上的例子，我們可以歸納成以下的規則：

（1）凡動詞是 "*verb to be*" 的，變成問句時，動詞移到主詞前面去。

原來句子	問句
You are a girl.	Are you a girl?
He was a teacher.	Was he a teacher?
They were all old.	Were they all old?
This song is beautiful.	Is this song beautiful?
Peter is a good student.	Is Peter a good student?

（2）動詞不是 "*verb to be*"，也沒有助動詞，改成問句時，必須加助動詞 "*do*" 或它的變形，這個助動詞必須在主詞的前面。

原來句子	問句
I like music.	Do I like music?
He likes sports.	Does he like sports?
Peter went to America.	Did Peter go to America?
He ate three apples last night.	Did he eat three apples last night?
Her mother calls her every week.	Does her mother call her every week?

（3）句子中間如已有助動詞，改成問句時，只要將助動詞移到主動詞前面即可。

原來句子	問句
He did not eat.	Did he eat?
He has gone to America.	Has he gone to America?
She can dance.	Can she dance?
I will see you tonight.	Will I see you tonight?
They are going to Washington.	Are they going to Washington?

我們的問句中，當然也可已有否定的意義，比方說，我們可以問：

　　你不喜歡音樂嗎？

　　他不是你的弟弟嗎？

　　你從未見過他？

英文句子也可以如此，例如：

1. Don't you like music?

2. Doesn't he play piano?

3. Aren't you his brother?

4. Isn't he a good student?

5. Didn't he go to school?

6. Hasn't he lived here?

7. Won't he leave tomorrow?

注意，這時"*not*"通常和動詞連在一起了。有一件事，是我們中國人必須注意的，假如有人問你：「你不喜歡音樂嗎」？而你本人的確也不喜歡音樂，你會回答說：「是，我不喜歡音樂」。也就是說，我們中國人的回答是順著問句的。問句說你不喜歡，我們同意他的說法，所以前面加一個「是」。假設我喜歡音樂，我會回答說：「不，我喜歡音樂」。

可是，英文正好相反，英文的"*yes*"和"*no*"，與問句的問法無關，而對應了回答的事實。舉例來說，我們的問句也許是：

Don't you like music?

你如不喜歡音樂就回答說：

No, I don't like music.

你如喜歡音樂，就回答說：

Yes, I like music.

再舉一例，有人問：

Isn't he Chinese?

如果他是中國人，就回答：

  "Yes, he is."

他如不是，就回答：

  "No, he isn't."

  反正，英文的"*yes*"和"*no*"，都和答案的事實對應，而與如何問無關。

練習二十五

將以下句子翻譯成英文問句:

1.你喜歡他嗎?

2.他是美國人嗎?

3.你昨天有沒有去教堂?

4.他曾經到過日本嗎?

5.你要去台北嗎?

6.他不喜歡體育嗎?

7.你從未去過日本嗎?

8.他有一個妹妹嗎?

9.他們都是學生嗎?

10.你的哥哥昨天見過我爸爸嗎?

7.2 回答不只是Yes和No的問句

問句的答案當然不一定只是"*yes*"或"*no*"，以下的問句都是例子：

1. Where did you buy this book?
2. Where did you see him?
3. How do you like America?
4. Whom do you like?
5. Which cake do you want?
6. Whose book is this?
7. What kind of method is this?
8. Which country were you born in?
9. Which do you want, an apple or an orange?
10. Whom do you like most, your brother or your sister?
11. Where did you go last night?
12. When did you meet your father?
13. When did you read this book?
14. Whom did you give this book to?

以上的問句中都有助動詞，但以下的問句中，助動詞是不存在的：

1. Who gave you this car?

2. Who wrote this letter?

3. Who took my pen away?

4. Who wants to go with me?

5. Who can sing this song?

練習二十六

將以下的中文問句翻譯成英文問句：

1.你在哪裡買這本書的？

2.他什麼時候到美國去的？

3.他爸爸的名字是什麼？

4.這是誰的書？

5.你從哪裡來的？

6.你要哪一本書？

7.這個孩子是誰？

8.他最喜歡誰？

9.他叫什麼名字？

10.你昨天到哪裡去了？

11.這是誰的狗？

練習二十七

填空：

1. _____ did you go last night?

2. _____ book do you like?

3. _____ is your brother?

4. _____ is his name?

5. _____ wrote this letter?

6. _____ did you give this book to?

7. _____ gave you this book?

8. _____ car is this?

9. _____ dog is this?

10. _____ movie did you see?

11. _____ can speak English?

12. _____ did you speak to?

13. _____ kind of car is this?

14. _____ fruit do you like most?

15. _____ does not swim?

第八章

被動語氣

8.1　及物動詞和不及物動詞

任何一個英文句子必定有一個動詞，請先注意以下例句的
動詞：

1. He was a teacher before.

2. He went to school yesterday.

3. He hit a dog.

4. I saw you yesterday.

5. He walks to school every day.

6. He sent this book to me.

7. They are good students.

8. He wrote two novels.

9. They ate all of the apples.

10. He swims every morning.

在以上的例子中，第3, 4, 6, 8及9句子中的動詞都是及物動詞(transitive verbs)。這些動詞後面都跟著一個名詞，而這個名詞是動詞的受詞(object)，其他句子的動詞，都是不及物動詞，因為他們都沒有任何受詞。

我們將以上句子中，主詞、及物動詞和受詞的關係分析如下：

句子	主詞	及物動詞	受詞
He hit a dog.	He	hit	dog
I saw you yesterday.	I	saw	you
He sent his book to me.	He	sent	his book
He wrote two novels.	He	wrote	two novels
They ate all of the apples.	They	ate	all of the apples

一旦動詞是及物動詞，我們就可以將這個句子由原來的主動語氣(active voice)改成被動語氣(passive voice)。但我們也要警告讀者，不要輕易用被動語氣，因為有時被動語氣的句子是不自然的。

8.2 沒有助動詞的被動語氣

在這以前，我們的句子都是主動語氣，這種句子的基本形式如下：

主詞＋動詞＋受詞

所謂被動語氣，乃是將原來的受詞變成主詞。舉例來說，主動語氣中，我們說「我看到一些狗」，在被動語氣中，我們說「一些狗被我看到」。在英文中，將主動語氣改成被動語氣，必須做以下的動作：

1. 原有受詞變成主詞。
2. 動詞變成 *verb to be*＋過去分詞（past participle）。
3. 原有主詞變成在動詞後面，但前面加 *"by"*。

舉例來說，主動語氣的句子可以是：

I saw a cat.

被動語氣就成了：

A cat was seen by me.

最重要的是，*"verb to be"* 的時式必須和原句子的相同，以上的例子中，動詞是過去式，所以 *"verb to be"* 也是過去式。除此以外，*"verb to be"* 也要配合新的主詞。請看以下的例子：

I saw two cats.

改成被動語氣以後，句子是：

> Two cats were seen by me.

以下是主動改被動的例子，最重要的是注意"*verb to be*"的形式：

主動語氣（active voice）	被動語氣（passive voice）
Mr. Jones hit the dog.	The dog was hit by Mr. Jones.
My brother saw you yesterday.	You were seen by my brother yesterday.
He sent the book to me.	The book was sent to me by him.
Dickens wrote those two novels.	Those two novels were written by Dickens.
They ate all of the apples.	All of the apples were eaten by them.
Jane wrote that song.	That song was written by Jane.
My mother loves me.	I am loved by my mother.

練習二十八

將以下的句子由主動語氣改成被動：

1. He saw that movie last night.

2. He wrote that letter to me.

3. He teaches those English classes.

4. God loves you.

5. They bought two houses.

6. I painted this room.

7. He grows those roses.

8. He helps his students.

9. I sold the house.

10. My uncle bought this car.

練習二十九

將以下的句子由被動語氣改成主動語氣：

1. The policeman was seen by me.

2. Those two books were written by me.

3. These sentences were corrected by my teacher.

4. He was hit by a car.

5. His door was locked by me.

6. His house was built by my father.

7. His boat was given to me by my father.

8. This bird is rarely seen by people here.

9. He is liked by everyone.

10. They were given ten dollars by their friends.

11. This picture was taken by him.

12. Too much wine was drunk by the young men.

13. I was taught by Mr. Wang.

14. He was helped by his father.

15. They were served by that waiter.

16. His food was prepared by my mother.

17. His toy was made by my sister.

18. The book was returned to me by Jim.

19. That song was written by my brother.

20. I was invited by him to a party.

8.3 有助動詞肯定句的被動語氣

在上一節，我們所有的例子都只是肯定句，句子中沒有助動詞，可是有些肯定句還是有助動詞的，以下是一些例子：

	主動語氣	被動語氣
現在進行式	I am writing this letter.	The letter is being written by me.
現在完成式	I have written the letter.	The letter has been written by me.
過去進行式	I was writing the letter when you came.	The letter was being written by me when you came.
過去完成式	I had written the letter before you came.	The letter had been written by me before you came.
未來式	I will write the letter.	The letter will be written by me.
未來完成式	I will have written this letter.	This letter will have been written by me.
未來式	I am going to see you.	You are going to be seen by me.

以下是更多的例子：

主動語氣	被動語氣
I have seen him.	He has been seen by me.
He is going to help you.	You are going to be helped by him.
He will teach English.	English will be taught by him.
He has helped me all my life.	I have been helped by him all my life.
He had called me before you came.	I had been called by him before you came.
He was calling his mother when we went there.	His mother was being called by him when we went there.

助動詞不一定和時式有關，"*can, should, has to*"等等都是助動詞，這些助動詞在改成被動語氣的時侯，都應維持原狀，只需加入"*verb to be*"和過去分詞即可。以下是一些例子：

主動語氣	被動語氣
I can play the piano.	The piano can be played by me.
I may use this room.	This room may be used by me.
He must give the book to me.	The book must be given to me by him.
You should help him.	He should be helped by you.

主動語氣	被動語氣
You have to write this letter.	This letter has to be written by you.
He ought to write this report.	This report ought to be written by him.

練習三十

將以下的句子改成被動語氣：

1. He has written three novels.

2. He will write that letter.

3. They will sing these songs tomorrow.

4. He will give the speech.

5. They are painting the house.

6. I have given him three books.

7. I can do this job.

8. He had told me that story before we went there.

9. The teachers should help the students.

10. He is writing the report now.

11. The students must read this book.

12. I have to give this letter to my mother tonight.

13. All citizens ought to obey the law.

14. He has eaten all of the cakes.

15. The reporters were taking pictures when the storm started.

16. He had finished the work before five o'clock last night.

17. Peter will write that letter.

18. John has received my letter.

19. Millions of people saw the movie Gone with the Wind.

20. He has proved that theorem.

練習三十一

將以下句子改成主動語氣：

1. Two books have been written by Joseph.

2. Football is being chosen by many students.

3. He should be given that lecture by his father.

4. That report will be written by him.

5. The letter has been received by the King.

6. This movie should be seen by everyone.

7. This book ought to be read by every student.

8. They are being helped by me.

9. The movie is going to be seen by all of us.

10. This cake can be eaten by kids.

8.4 否定句的被動語氣

將否定句或問句改成被動語氣，其步驟如下：

    a. 將此句子改成肯定句。

    b. 將此肯定句子改成被動語氣。

    c. 將此被動語氣的句子改成否定句。

現在舉一個否定的例子：I did not take this picture.

a. 對應的肯定句是：

I took this picture.

b. 改成被動語氣：

This picture was taken by me.

c. 再改成否定句：

This picture was not taken by me.

下面的例子都是用來解釋如何將否定句改成被動語氣：

1. They did not like the music.

    a. They liked the music.

    b. The music was liked by them.

    c. The music was not liked by them.

2. I have not written that letter.

    a. I have written that letter.

b. That letter has been written by me.

c. That letter has not been written by me.

3. You can not eat that cake.

    a. You can eat that cake.

    b. That cake can be eaten by you.

    c. That cake can not be eaten by you.

4. He does not play music.

    a. He plays that kind of music.

    b. That kind of music is played by him.

    c. That kind of music is not played by him.

5. I am not going to see you.

    a. I am going to see you.

    b. You are going to be seen by me.

    c. You are not going to be seen by me.

6. They will not see that movie.

    a. They will see that movie.

    b. That movie will be seen by them.

    c. That movie will not be seen by them.

7. They did not help me.

a. They helped me.

b. I was helped by them.

c. I was not helped by them.

8. I did not tell that story.

a. I told that story.

b. That story was told by me.

c. That story was not told by me.

　　在下面，我們將省略中間步驟，直接寫出一個否定句的被動語氣，英文好的人應該是不需要中間步驟的：

主動語氣	被動語氣
They do not enjoy such music.	Such music is not enjoyed by them.
He did not tell that story.	That story was not told by him.
They have not written that story.	That story has not been written by them.
Peter is going to see me.	I am not going to be seen by Peter.
He will not help me.	I will not be helped by him.
John will not eat that cake.	That cake will not be eaten by John.
I can not drink that wine.	That wine can not be drunk by me.

練習三十二

將以下的否定句改成被動語氣：

1. The farmers here do not grow apples.

2. He did not meet me last night.

3. I have not written that letter.

4. John is not going to see that movie.

5. I did not film that movie.

6. He does not speak English.

7. He will not speak English.

8. You should not eat that cake.

9. My mother does not eat that kind of fish.

10. John has not written that report.

練習三十三

將以下句子改成主動語氣：

1. The book was not written by him.

2. I am not going to be helped by you.

3. That book has not been received by John.

4. That song is not liked by college students.

5. John is not loved by Mary.

6. I will not be met by my student tomorrow.

7. Meat is not eaten by vegetarians.

8. The door was not opened by me.

9. That ten dollars were not paid by me.

10. The car was not bought by me.

8.5 問句的被動語氣

將問句改成被動語氣，步驟類似上一節的步驟，我們先將問句變成肯定句，然後將這個定句子變成被動語氣，最後在將這個被動語氣的句子變回，成為問句。

例如：Do young kids enjoy classical music?

a. 先改成肯定句：

Young kids enjoy classical music.

b. 再改成被動語氣：

Classical music is enjoyed by young kids.

c. 最後改成問句：

Is classical music enjoyed by young kids?

為了使讀者熟悉，我們在下面舉了很多的例子：

1. Did you eat that cake?

a. You ate that cake.

b. That cake was eaten by you.

c. Was that cake eaten by you?

2. Do farmers in Taiwan grow apples?

a. Farmers in Taiwan grow apples.

b. Apples are grown by farmers in Taiwan.

    c. Are apples grown by farmers in Taiwan?

3. Have you finished the report?

    a. You have finished the report.

    b. The report has been finished by you.·

    c. Has the report been finished by you?

4. When did you write that letter?

    a. You wrote that letter.

    b. That letter was written by you.

    c. When was the letter written by you?

5. Have you seen that movie?

    a. You have seen that movie.

    b. That movie has been seen by you.

    c. Has the movie been seen by you?

6. When did Stevenson write that novel?

    a. Stevenson wrote that novel.

    b. That novel was written by Stevenson.

    c. When was that novel written by Stevenson?

7. Is he painting his room?

    a. He is painting his room.

b. His room is being painted by him.

c. Is his room being painted by him?

在下面，我們將省略中間步驟，直接寫出一個問句的被動語氣，英文好的人應該是不需要中間步驟的：

主動語氣	被動語氣
Does he help his students?	Are his students helped by him?
Did he tell that story?	Was that story told by him?
Has she written that story?	Has that story been written by her?
Whom is Peter going to visit?	Who is going to be visited by Peter?
When did you read that book?	When was that book read by you?
Does he enjoy that song?	Is that song enjoyed by him?
Why do his friends avoid him?	Why is he avoided by his friends?
Whom did you see?	Who was seen by you?
Has he read that report?	Has that report been read by him?
Is he writing that letter?	Is that letter being written by him?

練習三十四

將以下句子改成被動語氣：

1. Is he writing a book?

2. Did he write that book?

3. Did you sign that letter?

4. Where did you see that movie?

5. When did you see that movie?

6. Has he finished that job?

7. Did Mother give you the gift?

8. Did your mother visit you last night?

9. Do they grow roses?

10. Do they speak English?

11. Did you win that game of tennis?

12. Will you teach English?

練習三十五

將以下句子改成主動語氣：

1. Was the cake eaten by you?

2. Is he liked by all of us?

3. Is that kind of music loved by everyone in Japan?

4. Is fish eaten by old people?

5. Are roses loved by most women?

6. Was he called by you?

7. Is soccer played by John?

8. When was this music written by Mozart?

9. When was he seen by you?

10. Were they seen by you last night?

練習三十六

將適宜的動詞填入：

1. I _____ (send) two letters yesterday. _____ (do)
   you _____ (receive) them? Every letter _____ (write)
   by me. Please _____ (write) back to me soon.

2. I _____ (invite) to a dancing party last week. The
   music _____ (be) so noisy. I _____ (leave) the party
   as early as I _____ (can).

3. Did you _____ (write) that report? Yes, it _____
   (write) by me.

4. He _____ (not like) music when he was a child.   After
   he _____ (get) into college, he _____ (teach) by a
   good music professor.   Now, he _____ (enjoy) music very
   much and _____ (listen) to classical music every morning.

5. I _____ (buy) a red car yesterday. It _____ (make) in
   Japan. It will _____ (deliver) to me tomorrow.

6. I _____ (not go) to school yesterday because my
   bicycle _____ (steal).

I _____ (buy) a new bike yesterday.

7. Where _____ (do) you go last night? I _____ (can)

not _____ (find) you.　You _____ (see) by no one.

8. A: _____ (do) he _____ (smoke)?

B: No, he _____ (do not). Smoking has never _____

(try) by him.

9. Was the book _____ (write) by him?

10. I _____ (buy) three books lately. One _____ (write)

by Graham Greene.

I _____ (finish) reading it.　There _____ (be) many

interesting stories in it.

練習三十七

改錯：

1. This is a book which wrote by Dickens.

2. Are the music enjoyed by those elderly people?

3. When are you visited by your father yesterday?

4. This book written by John.

5. He is invited to come to my home by my father yesterday.

6. This house is built in 1913.

7. This letter was wrote by him.

8. This letter has never finished.

9. Was you given a book?

10. I have never called by my father. I always call him first.

第九章
動詞如何轉換成名詞、動名詞和不定詞

9.1 問題的來源

　　對我們說中文的人而言，一個字究竟是動詞，還是名詞，其實是很少人知道的，對一般人而言，「唱歌」是動詞，但是如果我們說，「唱歌是有益的」，我們又發現「唱歌」其實也是名詞。「我愛唱歌」，這句話中，「唱歌」也是名詞。

　　英文就不同了，英文裡很少有一個字，又是動詞，又是名詞的，"*sing*"是動詞，絕不能當作名詞用。怪不得有很多中國人會說：

　　　* Sing is good for you.　或者是
　　　* I like sing.

　　既然"*sing*"是動詞，也沒有一個"*sing*"的名詞，怎麼辦呢？英文解套的辦法很有趣，他們用動名詞（gerund）和不定詞（infinitive）來將一個動詞改成一個名詞。

9.2 動名詞

　　所謂動名詞，乃是將一個動詞，字尾加上"*ing*"，一夕之間，這個動詞就可以當作名詞用了。請看以下的例子：

1. I like *singing*.
2. *Playing* basketball is good for you.
3. Do you enjoy *listening* to classical music?
4. Is *traveling* around the world meaningful to you?
5. *Studying* English is not difficult.

　　我們不妨將動名詞的用法分一下類：

（1）動名詞可用作主詞，如：

Playing tennis is enjoyed by many people.

Taking drugs is avoided by most people.

Being kind to others is important for every one.

Respecting your parents shows good character.

（2）動名詞可以用作動詞的受詞，如：

I enjoy *studying* English.

He does not mind *walking* long distances.

I have never enjoyed *being* alone in my life.

He loves *swimming*.

（3）動名詞可以用作介系詞（preposition）的受詞，英文裡有
很多介系詞，"*at, in, about, of, on*"等等都是介系詞，介系
詞後面必定跟一個名詞，也是它的受詞，舉例來說：

> on the table
>
> in my home
>
> about Hitler
>
> of my life
>
> on this island

各位一定注意到，每一個介系詞後面都有一個名詞，作
為它的受詞。

動名詞是可以作為介系詞的受詞的，如：

This book is about *traveling*.

He is responsible for *cleaning* the kitchen.

My brother is capable of *writing* programs.

You just keep on *going* straight.

在下面，我們要給各位更多有關動名詞的例子，各位不妨看看每一個句子中，那個動名詞是作什麼用的。

1. Instead of *swimming*, he walks every morning.

2. He likes *walking* in the woods.

3. Are you interested in *playing* tennis?

4. *Loving* is to be kind to others.

5. *Reading* is important to students.

6. In addition to *traveling*, he also likes *reading* novels.

7. You will be happy by *helping* others.

8. He is worried about *being* late.

9. I finished *writing* the report yesterday.

10. They thanked me for *lending* them money.

11. He has never finished *writing* the novel.

12. She is in charge of *teaching* English in our school.

13. My father objected to my *going* to the summer camp.

14. Please stop *joking* about my brother.

15. I look forward to *seeing* you.

16. He has never enjoyed *traveling*.

17. She was excited about *going* abroad.

18. I consider *gambling* a bad thing to do.

19. I have never dreamed of *flying* an airplane.

20. He suggested *talking* to our teacher.

21. I believe in *doing* some kind of exercise every day.

22. *Playing* the piano is no fun at all.

23. Nancy is accustomed to *sleeping* late.

24. Are you tired of *driving* for so long?

25. You should forgive others for *doing* wrong things.

26. He insists on *getting* up early every morning.

27. Thank you for *participating* in my concert.

28. He is used to *studying* alone.

29. They are not used to *speaking* English.

30. He is accustomed to *being* polite to others.

31. I object to *seeing* dirty movies.

32. You should take advantage of *studying* in such a good place.

練習三十八

改正以下的錯誤：

1. Play tennis is fun.

2. I hate swim.

3. Stop talk about me.

4. In addition to read interesting books, you should also watch
   TV from time to time.

5. I am not interested in swim.

6. He talks about go to America.

7. I believe in do exercise every day.

8. The cost of transfer a student to another school is very high.

9. Please forgive me for make this mistake.

10. Swim keeps me from getting cold.

練習三十九

填充，每一個句子填入一個介系詞和一個動名詞，先舉一個例子。

I am interested __in__ （listen）__listening__ to music.

1. Please forgive me _____ （be）_____ so late.

2. In addition _____ （study）_____ , you should also have some exercise every day.

3. We talked _____ （build）_____ a house next year.

4. Thank you _____ （help）_____ me.

5. He is excited _____ （travel）_____ to Japan.

6. I am looking forward _____ （meet）_____ you.

7. He insists _____ （talk）_____ to me personally.

8. I believe _____ （exercise）_____ every day.

9. Did you participate _____ that （swim）_____ match.

10. He was not used _____ （listen）_____ to

classical music.

11. My mother objected _____ (visit) _____ my
aunt tomorrow.

12. I am not accustomed _____ (go) _____ to
bed so late.

13. I am interested _____ (swim) _____.

14. Are you responsible _____ (write) _____
this report?

15. He is excited _____ (see) _____ me
tomorrow.

16. He is looking forward _____ (see) _____
that movie.

17. I am not used _____ (hear) _____ that kind
of noise.

18. You should take advantage _____ (have) _____
such a good family.

19. He is in charge _____ (send) _____ students
to other schools.

練習四十

將以下中文句子譯成英文句子：

1. 我不喜歡跳舞。

2. 你對游泳有興趣嗎？

3. 打籃球是有趣的。

4. 我們昨天談到(talk about)教英文的事。

5. 我不習慣(be not used to)抽煙。

6. 我反對(object to)在公開場合哭泣(cry in public)。

7. 除了游泳以外，他還應該打棒球(用in addition to)。

8. 他可以(be capable of)每天跑一公里。

9. 他負責(be in charge of)找尋一個好的地方。

10. 我已習慣了(be accustomed to)早起。

9.3 不定詞

「不定詞＝*to*＋動詞的原式」。例如"*to go, to love, to eat*"等等，都是不定詞，不定詞和動名詞的用法相似，以下全是用不定詞用作名詞的例子：

To love is to forgive.

To forgive your enemies will make you happy.

I like *to eat* chicken.

I asked my brother *to come* here.

He continued *to read*.

也許讀者發現了不定詞和動名詞不同的地方，不定詞不能用在介系詞的後面，以下的句子都是錯的：

*I am interested in to play piano.

*He is worried about to go abroad.

*I am in charge of to prepare for the party.

如何將不定詞用成名詞呢？

(1)不定詞可以用作主詞，如：

To play tennis is great fun.

To play safe in the stock market is necessary.

To be kind to others is important for every one.

To respect your parents shows good character.

(2)不定詞可以用成很多動詞的受詞：

I like *to swim*.

He loves *to listen* to jokes.

My brother loves *to be* different.

I agree *to lend* him money.

Do you like *to sing*?

(3)不定詞可以跟在代名詞的後面，形式如下：

動詞＋不直接受詞＋直接受詞(不定詞)

例如：

I told *him to work* hard.

I asked *my brother to come* back home.

He expects *his friends to help* him.

My teacher told *me to wait* for him.

I invited *my sister to go* to see a movie.

(4)不定詞常用在上述句子的被動語氣中，例如：

He was told *to work* hard.

My brother was asked *to come* back home.

His friend is expected *to help* me.

I was told by my teacher *to wait*.

My sister was invited *to go* to see a movie.

以下是更多的不定詞例子：

To give is more meaningful than *to receive*.

I love *to swim* in cold weather.

He agreed *to listen* to my story.

He decided *to go* anyway.

I told him *to buy* my book.

I invited him *to come* to my house.

I asked him *to cook* for me tonight.

Students are asked *to work* hard.

He needs *to work* hard.

I want you *to send* this letter to my father.

He requires every student *to read* one novel every week.

Every student is required *to read* one novel every week.

　　讀者一定會問，是不是動名詞可以和不定詞互調？答案是否定的，有些動詞後面可以跟動名詞和不定詞，但也有些動詞，後面只能跟動名詞，有些動詞後面只能跟不定詞。

　　有些動詞後面可以跟動名詞或不定詞，如*"love, like,*

hate, start, begin"

　　以下的動詞，後面只能跟動名詞：

Enjoy	I enjoy *eating* good food.
appreciate	I appreciate your *being* kind to others.
avoid	You should avoid *making* mistakes.
keep on	Keep on *working* hard.
keep	Keep *singing*.
consider	He considered *leaving* home.
finish	He finished *writing* this book.
suggest	May I suggest *drinking* a cup of coffee?
discuss	We discussed *traveling* to New Zealand.

　　以下的動詞正好相反，只能跟不定詞：

agree	I agree *to sign* this letter.
plan	He plans *to go* away.
want	They want *to rent* a car.
decide	He decided *to work* hard.
seem	He seems *to be* very happy.
appear	He appears *to be* very sad.

一個字非常特殊，必須討論一下，那就是"*stop*"：

　　　　stop smoking　指不再抽煙了

　　　　stop to smoke　指停下來，開始抽煙

9.4 動名詞和不定詞的被動和否定形式

　　將動詞改成名詞的時候，也可以有被動語氣和否定語氣，以下是一些例子：

> Everyone likes *to be loved*.
>
> This cup needs *to be washed*.
>
> *Being trusted* is important.
>
> I told him *not to leave* this house.
>
> He asked me *not to cry*.
>
> I was told *not to fall* asleep in class.
>
> *To be given* a good gift on Christmas Eve makes me happy.
>
> *Being invited* to that party is a great honor to me.

練習四十一

將下面的空格填入動名詞或不定詞

1. I enjoy _____ (listen) to rock and roll music.

2. I asked him _____ (go) away.

3. He was asked _____ (leave).

4. I suggest _____ (have) some fun.

5. He seems _____ (be) a kind person.

6. You appear _____ (be) quite tired.

7. I told him _____ (have) a cup of wine.

8. I invited him _____ (come) over.

9. Everyone of you is required _____ (work) hard.

10. Do you like _____ (swim)?

11. I ordered him _____ (read) my book.

12. I was expected _____ (write) a letter to you.

13. He asked me _____ (read) this letter to him.

14. Please keep _____ (talk) to me.

15. Stop _____ (drive) so fast. It is dangerous to drive too fast.

16. I hate _____ (smoke).

17. _____ (pass) the test is important.

18. _____ (work) hard is the key to success.

19. My wife asked me to _____ (bring) some flowers home.

20. He avoided _____ (tell) lies.

練習四十二

將以下中文句子譯成英文句子,用動名詞或不定詞。

1.我請(invite)他到我家來。

2.我教(teach)他游泳。

3.被人愛令人快樂。

4.我討厭(hate)抽煙。

5.我們應該避免(avoid)飲煙。

6.不要再(stop)抽煙了。

7.每個人都期待(expect)他寫一本好書。

8.我要求(require)他每天唸英文。

9.5 不定詞的簡式

不定詞中一定要有"*to*"，但在有幾個動詞的後面，"*to*"又要省掉，最著名的是"*let*"，我們絕不可以說：

　　*I let him to leave.

而一定要說：

　　I let him leave.

我們也不能說：

　　* I made him to work hard.

　　（我使他努力工作。）

而一定要說：

　　I made him work hard.

以下的動詞後面，不定詞的後面都要省掉"*to*"。

動詞	例句
let	My mother let me watch TV tonight.
make	He makes his students respect teachers.
have	He had his sons clean their rooms.
see	I saw him run away.
hear	I heard the birds sing.
watch	I watched the kids play.
notice	I noticed her cry.

　　因爲在這些動詞的後面，本來應該用不定詞，僅僅是
"to"被省掉了，因此我們在這些動詞的後面仍然要用原式，
以下的句子都是錯的：

　　　*He made his son ran away from home.
　　　*I saw him walked away. .
　　　*I have never heard him sang any song.

　　"help"這一個動詞非常特別，它後面的不定詞中的"to"
可省略也可不省，以下的句子都是對的：

　　I helped him wash his car.
　　I helped him to wash his car.

練習四十三

以下的句子都有錯，請改正：

1. He lets his son to drive his car.

2. He made me felt happy.

3. I made my friend to discuss his problem with me.

4. I had my son to get up early every morning.

5. I helped my father painted his house.

6. I had my brother to carry this heavy luggage for me.

7. I had Mary to marry me.

8. This song makes everyone to cry.

9. I helped Nancy worked hard.

10. He made us to believe him.

11. I saw him to play.

12. I heard Mary sang several songs.

13. I watched her to swim.

14. I saw the birds to fly away.

第十章
如何將動詞改成形容詞

　　我們中文裡，一個字有時是動詞，有時卻又可以用作形容詞，最著名的例子是「微笑老蕭」（前行政院長蕭萬長的外號），「微笑」應該是動詞，可是在這裡，顯然「微笑」是形容詞。「哭泣」通常是動詞，可是我們也可以說「哭泣的孩子」。也難怪我們常見到以下錯誤的英文句子：

　　　　*a smile face

　　　　*a run boy

需知"*smile*"和"*cry*"都是動詞，是不能當作形容詞來用的。

　　可是，更糟糕的是以下句子：「住在台灣的人很有錢」，我們很多人會說：

　　　　*People live in Taiwan are rich.

　　以上的話為什麼錯呢？因為"*people*"是主詞，"*are*"是動詞，"*live in Taiwan*"形容"*people*"，可是"*live*"是一個動詞，不能

用作形容詞的。怎麼辦呢？我們可以將一個動詞用成一個形容詞，我們的做法是利用分詞（participle）或不定詞（infinitive），而分詞有兩種：現在分詞（present participle）和過去分詞（past participle），我們在下一節，先談現在分詞的用法。

10.1 現在分詞作為形容詞

任何一個動詞，都有一個現在分詞（present participle），現在分詞的形式是在動詞後面加上"*ing*"，如：

> laughing
>
> crying
>
> walking
>
> swimming
>
> running

以下的例子中，現在分詞都是形容詞

> a *crying* baby
>
> a *smiling* girl
>
> an *exciting* story
>
> *running* water
>
> a *running* boy
>
> a *rising* star

現在分詞不一定放在名詞的前面，在以下的句子中，現在分詞都在名詞的後面：

a person *walking* in the woods

the young man *running* very fast

people *living* in Taiwan

the person *driving* that red car

the singer *singing* the national anthem（國歌）

the boys *playing* in the fields

the young boy *swimming* in the pool

以下句子中的現在分詞，都被用作形容詞。

1. We have a *crying* baby here.

2. Seeing is *believing*. （believing是形容詞，seeing是名詞）

3. Loving is *forgiving*.

4. He always wears a *smiling* face.

5. *Running* water is important for mankind.

6. Look at the *rising* sun.

7. The person *swimming* in that cold river is quite strong.

8. The young man *driving* the red car is rich.

9. Those boys *playing* basketball are happy.

10. This movie is *exciting*.

11. This news is very *upsetting*.

12. This story is *troubling*.

13. The young boy *swimming* in the pool is my brother.

14. People *living* in the United States consume more energy than other people.

15. The person *painting* the house there is from Mexico.

16. She has a *loving* husband.

17. He is a *rising* star.

練習四十四

將以下的中文句子譯成英文，每句都要用現在分詞

1.這是一本有趣的故事。

2.這門課很無聊(boring)。

3.看那隻在唱歌的鳥。

4.那位微笑的人是我的哥哥。

5.住在鄉下的人通常很健康。

6.我不認識那位騎腳踏車的男孩子。

7.那位正在吃冰淇淋的小孩子是我的兒子。

8.那位在問問題的學生非常聰明。

9.你見過那位打籃球的男孩子嗎？

10.那位垂死(dying)的病人是我的老師。

10.2 過去分詞作為形容詞

在完成式中，我們要用過去分詞，過去分詞也可以作為形容詞，以下是一些例子：

a *broken* window（破碎的窗）

a *fallen* angel（墮落的天使）

a *fallen* star（已經不走紅的明星）

a *depressed* person（一個沮喪的人）

a much *appreciated* action（為人很欣賞的動作）

究竟過去分詞和現在分詞何不同呢？過去分詞多半有被動和已經完成的意思。最好的例子是：開發中國家叫做 "a developing country"；已開發國家就叫做"a developed country"。

以下的例子可以解釋過去分詞和現在分詞的不同：

1. (a)這本書很有趣。

   This book is interesting.

   (b)我對這本書很有興趣。

   I am interested in this book.

2. (a)這是一部令人沮喪的電影。

   This is a depressing movie.

   (b)我看了這部電影以後，感到非常沮喪。

I felt very much depressed after seeing that movie.

3. (a)結果令人失望。

The result is frustrating.

(b)他因這個結果而非常失望。

He was frustrated because of the result.

4. (a)這個消息真令人難過。

This news is really upsetting.

(b)他們都很難過。

They are all upset.

5. (a)約翰的進步令人鼓舞。

John's progress is encouraging.

(b)我因約翰的進步而感到鼓舞。

I am encouraged by John's progress.

6. (a)水在燒。

The water is boiling.

(b)這是燒開的水。

This is boiled water.

7. (a)這個消息出人意外。

This news is surprising.

(b)我對這個消息感到意外。

I was surprised by the news.

8. (a)他的談話令人困惑。

His words are confusing.

(b)他是一個充滿困惑的人。

He is a confused person.

記住，以下的句子都是錯的：

*His statements are confused to me.

*I am interesting in music.

*He is an interested person.

*This is indeed a surprised news.

*This news is encouraged.

正確的句子應該是：

1. His statements are *confusing*.

2. I am *interested* in music.

3. He is an *interesting* person.

4. This is indeed a *surprising* news.

5. This news is *encouraging*.

以下是含有過去分詞的句子，每一個過去分詞都用作形容詞：

1. America is a *developed* country.

2. I found that dog *killed* in a car accident.

3. The *frustrated* student needs help.

4. I want the report *completed* before midnight.

5. He is totally *depressed*.

6. They are all *frustrated*.

7. The car *driven* by that young man is a Cadillac.

8. This book, *read* by almost every one, was written by Charles Dickens.

9. This is still an *unrealized* dream.

10. Are you *interested* in music?

11. I am really *surprised* to meet you.

12. I was *excited* by his arrival.

13. The girl *dressed* in white is from Japan.

14. A *depressed* person needs love from others.

15. Millions got *killed* in the Second World War.

16. He is a *troubled* child who needs advice.

17. I have a *broken* leg.

18. *Broken* glass is all over the place.

千萬注意，我們不可以輕易亂用過去分詞，以下的句子都
是錯的：

　　　*He is suffered.

　　　*This article will be appeared in the next issue of Science.

正確的說法是：

　　1.He suffers.

　　2.This article will appear in the next issue of Science.

練習四十五

將以下的中文句子譯成英文：

1.我對音樂有興趣。

2.這部人人都看過的電影是在好萊塢製作的。

3.他來自一個破碎的家庭。

4.這個國家的法律已經崩潰(break down)了。

5.我因這個消息而感到興奮。

6.我們應該幫助那位沮喪的學生。

7.三個人死於(get killed)這場車禍。

8.這是一個充滿了困惑的學生。

9.他是一個很有趣的人。

練習四十六

填空，全部用現在分詞或過去分詞：

1. He is totally _____ (confuse).

2. I am _____ (interest) in seeing that movie.

3. This movie is really _____ (excite).

4. That is a _____ (break) promise.

5. He has a _____ (break) arm.

6. Their marriage was _____ (break) up.

7. Justice is still not a _____ (realize) dream.

8. He is a _____ (depress) person.

9. The bicycle _____ (ride) by the young kid is mine.

10. I do not like to see any person _____ (injure).

11. I was very much _____ (surprise) to hear that news.

12. His statements are _____ (encourage).

13. The man _____ (talk) about Hitler is a professor.

14. The man _____ (pilot) the airplane is quite young.

15. The company _____ (manage) by Mr. Lee is getting better
and better.

16. Poor John now has a _____ (break) heart.

17. There are boys and girls _____ (dance) in the garden.

18. The _____ (steal) jacket has been found.

19. The boy _____ (laugh) there is not my son.

20. He has a _____ (smile) face.

21. This is indeed very _____ (excite).

22. This song, _____ (hear) by almost everyone, was written

by me.

23. I don't like the song _____ (write) by the Beatles.

24. She is a _____ (care) woman.

10.3 不定詞作為形容詞和副詞

不定詞可以用作名詞，也可以用作形容詞，以下都是不定詞用作形容詞的例子，要注意的是不定詞不會放在名詞的前面：

1. You don't have the right *to talk* so loudly.

2. He is *to blame*.

3. To see is *to believe*. ("To see"是名詞，"to believe"是形容詞。)

4. My job is *to teach* poor kids to learn.

5. We all have the duty *to serve* our country.

6. He has a talent *to sing*.

7. I don't have time *to play*.

8. He is a person *to be liked* by us all.

9. This is a book *to be read* by all students.

10. He has no money *to spend*.

11. This is not a good place for kids *to grow* up in.

12. This law is *to protect* innocent citizens.

13. I am glad *to see* you.

14. He is ready *to start* a war.

15. He is rich enough *to buy* the entire building.

16. They are afraid *to die*.

17. He has no right *to kill* anyone.

12. John is too weak *to do* this job.

13. My mother is too old *to drive* a car.

14. It is easy *to fall* behind in school.

練習四十七

將以下句子改成英文:

1. 我們都有納稅的義務。

2. 我們都有保持緘默(remain silent)的權利。

3. 他有游泳的天才。

4. 我已無錢可花。

5. 我無處可去。

6. 他太累了,不能開車了。(too... to...)

7. 我很高興看到你。

8. 他夠聰明,可以進入大學。(enough... to...)

9. 我的工作是教小孩英文。

10. 我看到你,感到很意外。(surprised to...)

11. 我們有很多可談的事。

12. 他沒有可以交談的朋友。

第十一章
片語和子句

請看以下的句子，特別注意斜體字群：

1. *Understanding* English is easy.
2. I want you *to work* hard.
3. Peter, *who has been to England*, speaks good English.
4. I told him that I was going away.

"*Understanding English*"和"*to work hard*"有一共同特色，他們都沒有主詞，也沒有動詞，這種字群，叫做片語(phrase)。

"Who has been to England"和"I was going away"中，內部都有主詞和動詞，這種字群，叫子句(clause)。

由於我們已經對片語很熟悉，我們在這裡不再討論，而我們在這一章將多多介紹子句的用法。

11.1 問題型式的名詞子句

　　假如我們說「我不知道他住在哪裡」，或者「他究竟住在哪裡仍是個謎」，我們就可以用這種問題型式的名詞子句，每一個名詞子句都要用"*who, where, whether, which*"等來開始。以下是典型的例子：

1. I don't know *where he came from.*

　（我不知道他來自何處。）

2. *Whether or not he is an American* is still a secret.

　（他是否是個美國人仍然是個秘密。）

3. I will find out *where he is living.*

　（我要找出他住在哪裡。）

4. I can not remember *whether he smokes or not.*

　（我不記得他是否吸煙。）

5. Please let me know *how old he is.*

　（請讓我知道他多大年紀。）

6. Kindly tell me *what you really need.*

　（請讓我知道你需要什麼。）

7. You have to decide *which book you want to buy.*

（你應該決定買哪一本書。）

8. Do you know *where he is from?*

（你知道他是從哪裡來的？）

9. Do you know *who he is?*

（你知道他是誰嗎？）

10. Please ask your brother *whether he is coming or not.*

（請問你的兄弟他會不會來。）

11. *When she is coming* remains a puzzle.

（她何時來仍然是個謎。）

12. I don't know *what he is interested in.*

（我不知道他的興趣何在。）

13. I don't understand *what he is talking about.*

（我不知道他在談什麼。）

14. Do you know *whose bicycle this is?*

（你知道這輛腳踏車是誰的嗎？）

15. Do you know *which country Hawaii belongs to?*

（你知道夏威夷屬於哪一個國家嗎？）

16. You should ask your mother *where you were born.*

（你應該問你的母親你在哪裡生的。）

　　雖然每一個名詞都有問題的意義，我們卻不能在名詞子句中用問句的型式，因爲畢竟這個名詞子句僅僅是一個子句而已，它的結尾並不是"？"。

　　因此以下的句子都是錯的：

　　　　*I don't know where did he come from.

　　　　*I will find out how old is he.

　　　　*Kindly tell me what do you need.

　　　　*You have to decide which book do you want to buy.

　　　　*When is he coming remains a puzzle.

練習四十八

將以下的中文句子譯成英文:

1.我不知道你是誰。

2.請告訴我你是否是美國人。

3.我不記得你是否喝咖啡。

4.請問你的姊姊她去年是否去過日本。

5.你知道他是誰嗎?

6.他從哪裡來的是一個謎(puzzle)。

7.我要找出他哥哥會不會游泳。

8.我知道他為何如此悲傷。

9.你知道瑪麗什麼時候來嗎?

10.你知道發生了什麼事嗎?

11.我知道天空為什麼是藍的。

12.請告訴我你去年去哪裡工作的。

13.你知道他在談什麼嗎？

14.我不懂他的問題是什麼。

練習四十九

改錯：

1. Please tell me *why is he so sad.*

2. I do not know *where is she from.*

3. Please tell me *how many people are there in this house.*

4. Let me know *how old are you.*

5. *Is he Japanese* is a mystery.

6. Do you know *who is the president of the United States*?

7. May I ask you *which kind of coffee do you like*?

8. I can not remember *how old am I.*

9. *What is he talking about* is unclear to me.

10. Do you know *why is he coming*?

練習五十

選擇適當的代名詞，如"*whether, which, what, who, how, when, why*"等填入下面句子的空格(有時會有多種正確的填法)：

1. I don't know _____ book you bought.

2. Do you know _____ he is from?

3. Please ask him _____ he drinks tea or not.

4. _____ he is thinking about is well known to all of us.

5. Let me guess _____ old you are.

6. May I ask _____ you are so sad?

7. I don't know _____ he is.

8. Do you know _____ house this is?

9. This is not _____ I want.

10. I don't care _____ you are.

11.2 以that開始的名詞子句

現在我們先試著翻譯以下的句子：

地球是圓的是眾所周知的事。

一種直接了當的翻譯是：

The earth is round is known to everyone.

遺憾的是，以上的句子是不對的，我們必須加一個"*that*"
到名詞子句裡去，以下的翻譯是正確的：

That the earth is round is known to everyone.

我們再來翻譯一個中文句子：

我要求他一定要用功唸書。

直接了當的翻譯可能像下面的：

*I demand he must work hard.

這是錯的，我們應該加一個*that*在這個名詞子句的前面。以
下的翻譯才是正確的：

I demand that he must work hard.

雖然我們常看到這種"*that*"被省略的情形，我們仍希望大家
知道，為保險起見，最好不要省掉"*that*"。以下是一些例子：

1. That the sun rises from the west is wrong.

（太陽從西方升起是錯的。）

2. That a lot of Jews were killed during the Second World War is now a historical fact.

（大批猶太人在第二次大戰中被殺是歷史上的事實。）

3. I didn't know that he is such a diligent student.

（我不知道他是如此勤快的學生。）

4. I demand that you go away.

（我要求你離開。）

5. I suggest that you go swimming every morning.

（我建議你每天早上游泳。）

6. That we should all respect our parents should be taught to our kids.

（我們該教孩子們尊敬父母。）

7. I don't think that he is a good athlete.

（我不認為他是一個好運動員。）

8. Do you think that she is a good actress?

（你認為她是一個好的演員嗎？）

9. That he can speak good English helps him.

（他能說很好的英文，這點對他很有幫助。）

10. I propose that we get married.

（我建議我們結婚。）

11. Let us always remember that there are a lot of poor people in the world.

（我們永遠記住世界上有很多窮人。）

12. Never forget that we should always love one another.

（不要忘記我們應該互相友愛。）

13. I am surprised to find out that he is a Catholic.

（我很驚訝地發現他是個天主教徒。）

14. That we lost the game made all of us frustrated.

（我們輸了，這件事令我們大感沮喪。）

15. I can hardly believe that his English is so good.

（我不能相信他的英文如此之好。）

練習五十一

請將"that"加到以下句子去：

1. I told you you must leave.

2. I am glad you are here now.

3. He is an American is unknown to us.

4. Can you imagine he is Chinese?

5. Do you think he is Chinese?

6. Hitler was defeated in the Second World War is an important

   event in the history of mankind.

7. I do not think he is a bad student.

8. I am surprised to know she is from Japan.

9. It is hard to imagine he does not have a high school diploma.

10. Do you believe he is innocent?

11. I demand my students work hard.

12. The sun rises in the east is a fact.

練習五十二

將以下句子翻譯成英文(用"that"或"whether"):

1.我不相信他是我的哥哥。

2.我勸(advise)他到美國去。

3.你相信地球是圓的嗎?

4.我告訴他他一定要讀這本書。

5.我忘記了你是個小孩。

6.你能相信我會講英文(speak English)嗎?

7.他沒有來令我生氣(make me angry)。

8.我認為他是個好人。

9.不要忘記世界上有很多窮人。

10.我知道他教英文。

11.我從不知道他如此聰明。

12.我知道他不能來。

13.我希望他能來。

14.你相不相信他在台灣長大的？

15.我無法決定他該不該唸大學。

16.你告訴我他去年到美國了。

17.這位老師不知道我的爸爸也是老師。

18.我要問他明天會不會來我家。

19.你知道這火車到台北嗎？

20.請告訴我你會不會說英文。

11.3 形容詞子句

在上二節，子句都是用作名詞的。在這一節，我們要介紹一種新的子句，那就是形容詞子句。請看以下的中文句子：

住在那房子裡的人是我的哥哥。

我們不能直接了當地將以上的句子譯成：

*The person live in that house is my brother.

第一種辦法是將 "*live in the house*" 改成 "*living in the house*"，也就是說，我們可以將那個中文句子譯成下列的形式：

The person *living in the house* is my brother.

以上的句子中，"*living in the house*" 是一個片語，我們可以將這個片語改成子句。因此，以下的翻譯是正確的：

The person *who lives in the house* is my brother.

在以上的句子中 "*who lives in the house*" 是一個子句，因為它有主詞，也有動詞。他的作用是形容 "*The person*"，所以是一個形容詞子句。

由於形容詞子句永遠都是在形容一個名詞，因此我們在這個子句中必需有一個代名詞（pronoun），像 "*who, when, where, whom*" 等。

　　以下是一些形容詞子句的例子，讀者應該弄清楚每一個形容詞子句所形容的名詞。

1. The people *who live in the country* are often very healthy.
（住在鄉下的人常常很健康。）

2. Do you like people *who always talk about themselves*.
（你喜歡那些永遠講他自己的人嗎？）

3. The house *which we bought last year* is located beside a lake.
（我們去年買的房子座落在湖邊。）

4. I met your uncle *who has a red car*.
（我遇見了你那位有紅色汽車的叔叔。）

5. Do you know the author *who wrote this novel*?
（你知道寫這本小說的作者嗎？）

6. I have been to the house *where Charles Dickens lived*.
（我曾去過狄更斯住過的房子。）

7. I don't remember the year *when the Second World War broke out*.
（我不記得二次世界大戰哪一年爆發的。）

8. Let me know the date *when you got married*.
（讓我知道你是哪一天結婚的。）

9. I bought the car *which Michael Johnson drove*.
（我買下了麥克強森開的車子。）

10. The storm *which hit India* last week is very strong.
（上週襲擊印度的暴風雨是很強烈的。）

11. I thank all of you *who helped me*.
（我要謝謝所有幫助過我的人。）

12. The girl *whom you met last night* works in a library.
（你昨晚碰到的女孩子在一個圖書館裡工作。）

13. The students *whom you taught* like you very much.
（那些你教過的學生很喜歡你。）

14. I like the professor *who taught me English*.
（我喜歡那位教我英文的老師。）

15. In this country, there are a lot of students *who go to school by bus*. （這個國家有很多學生搭乘公車上學。）

16. Have you heard about the murder case *that occurred last night*?
（你有沒有聽到昨天晚上發生的謀殺案？）

17. Those *who love others* will be loved by others.
（愛人者人恆愛之。）

18. He is a person *whom everyone is talking about* these days.

（他是大家最近在討論的人。）

19. The party *which I went to* is interesting.

（我去參加的宴會很有趣。）

20. The professor *whom I spoke to* is very friendly.

（這位我和他談話的教授很和善。）

21. Russia, *which this island belongs to*, is a big country.

（這個島嶼屬於俄國，俄國是一個大的國家。）

　　請注意以上最後的四個句子，它們有一個共同的特性，那就是子句的最後一個字是一個介系詞（preposition），我們先看第一個句子：

He is a person whom everyone is talking about these days.

這一句話可以分成兩個句子來講：

He is a person.

Everyone is talking about him these days.

因此我們將這兩句話合併而成為：

He is a person whom everyone is talking about these days.

在正式的英文中，我們必須說：

He is a person about whom everyone is talking these days.

再看下一句：

The party *which I went* to is interesting.

這句話也可以分成兩句來講：

The party is interesting.

I went to the party.

因此我們將兩個句子合併為一個句子：

The party *which I went to* is interesting.

正式的講法應該是：

The party *to which I went* is interesting.

同理，在正式英文中，其他二個名詞子句中的介系詞，也應該放到前面去：

The professor *to whom I spoke* is very friendly.

Russia, *to which this island belongs*, is a big country.

我們還有一點必須在此指出，請看以下錯誤的句子：

*I like the book which you gave it to me.

以上句子中的"*it*"是多餘的，因為"*gave*"的受詞是"*which*"，不需要加"*it*"。

以下的句子都是錯的：

*He is the person whom everyone loves *him*.

*He is not the person whom you saw *him*.

練習五十三

將以下句子譯成英文(用形容詞子句):

1.我見到那位開快車的孩子。

2.我們在討論那些有問題的學生。

3.每天游泳的人一定很強壯。

4.開車送我去火車站的人是我的學生。

5.你所看到的女孩子是我的妹妹。

6.我喜歡你所寫的詩。

7.你們談到的那位教授是我的哥哥。

8.你們所聽到的音樂是藍調韻律(R & B)。

9.我喜歡那些有圖畫的書。

10.我不知道林肯在哪一個城市出生的。

11.我很喜歡你送我的CD。

12.我昨晚看的電影很無聊(boring)。

練習五十四

改錯：

1. I saw the man who you talked about.

2. He is not the man who we met.

3. Those cry very often are usually not liked.

4. I like to talk to people which are friendly.

5. I enjoy reading the book which you gave it to me.

6. Do you know the person which everyone knows?

7. Peter is a good singer practices singing everyday.

8. Do you know the Peter who we talked about?

9. Did you see the person who I spoke to?

10. I have seen the person whom we talked about him.

練習五十五

將代名詞如"who", "whom", "when", "where", "which"等填入空格：

1. He is the man _____ is very good at English.

2. I don't know the person _____ you talked to.

3. This is not the house _____ the president lives.

4. I do not like anyone _____ cries frequently.

5. Did you read the book, _____ you bought last month?

6. Do you know the year _____ the Second World War ended?

7. Do you know that student _____ I taught?

8. I have no idea about the person _____ you are talking about.

9. Do you know _____ he is talking about?

10. Do you know _____ dress it is?

第十二章
冠詞

假設我們要翻譯以下的中文句子：他是聰明的孩子。也許我們會將以上的句子翻譯成以下的句子：

*He is clever boy.

這種翻譯是錯的，"*boy*"的前面，必須有一個冠詞，英文冠詞只有兩個："*a*"和"*the*"，在這個例子，我們應該加"*a*"，因此正確的翻譯是：

He is *a* clever boy.

我們現在再看以下的中文句子：

他是昨天來看我的孩子。

以下的翻譯是錯的：

*He is boy who came to see me yesterday.

為什麼錯呢？仍然是在於"*boy*"前面沒有冠詞，這次我們必須加"*the*"，正確的翻譯是：

He is *the* boy who came to see me yesterday.

一般來說，英文句子的單數名詞前面都會有冠詞，沒有冠詞是例外，以下的句子都是錯的：

*He saw *cat*.

*I have *dog*.

*This is *car*.

King of England died last night.

*He is *professor* who taught me when I was young.

正確的句子是：

1. He saw *a* cat.

2. I have *a* dog.

3. This is *a* car.

4. *The* King of England died last night.

5. He is *the* professor who taught me when I was young.

我們知道大多數的名詞前面要加冠詞，但究竟要加 "*a*"，還是"*the*"呢？我們在下一節討論。

12.1 a和the的不同

"a"和"the"最大的不同，在於"a"後面的名詞不是指定的，而"the"後面的名詞是有所指的。我們不妨看以下的兩個句子，他們都是正確的，但意義卻不同。

John is *a* boy.

John is *the* boy.

"*John is a boy.*"的意思是「約翰是一個男孩」，而"*John is the boy.*"就一定有別的句子了，我們一定曾經提到過某一個男孩子，而約翰就是那個男孩子。可能的情形是：

There is a boy who is very good in mathematics.　John is *the* boy.

或者　John is *the* boy whom we talked about.

我們就以「國王」為例，如果我們泛指一般的國王，我們可以用複數，也可以用單數，但必須用"a"，以下是一些例子：

1. Kings are also human beings.

2. Even *a* king will die sooner or later.

3. Have you ever met *a* king？

4. He is an ordinary person, not *a* king.

如果我們的國王是指某一個特定的國王，就必須用 "*the*"，

舉一個例子,如果我們說「國王萬歲」,我們當然是指我們的國王,因此「國王萬歲」的翻譯就是

Long live *the* King.

以下的例子都是正確:

1. Here comes *the* King.

2. *The* King is a popular person in our country.

3. Even *the* King of England can not come in.

讀者應該了解,同類型的句子,可以用"*a*",也可以用"*the*",但意義是完全不同的,請看以下的句子:

He is not *a* boy who would cheat others.

意思是:

他不是那種會欺騙別人的男孩子。

再看以下的句子:

He is not *the* boy who cheated in the examination yesterday.

他不是昨天在考試中舞弊的男孩。

再看以下的句子:

He is *a* king.   他是一個國王。

如果說:

He is *the* King.

意思就完全不同了，這句話的意思是「他是我們國家的國王」，或者在另一個句子中，我們曾經提到過他是某某國家的國王。

請注意，世界上國王有好多個，如果我們僅僅說他是一個國王，當然沒有指定哪一個國家的國王，就用"*a king*"，如果我們用"*the King*"意思當然指我們共識中的國王。這時的"*king*"中的"*K*"必須大寫，以示尊敬。

我們再舉一個例子：
Please open *a* window.
是指請開一扇窗子，隨便哪一扇都可以。

Please open *the* window.
就不同了，說這句話的人和聽這句話的人一定有一個共識，"***the window***"一定是指某一扇特定的窗子，也許這間房子裡只有一扇窗，也可能他們談話中曾經提到某一扇窗，"***the window***"就是指那一扇窗。

我們可以再舉一個例，假如我們說，「我們需要一場大雨」，我們說：
We need *a* heavy rain.

如果我們說，「這場雨好大」，我們說：
The rain is really heavy.

有了這個基本觀念以後，我們就很容易了解以下句子中，爲什麼要用"*the*"：

I am going to *the* train station.

The post office is quite near.

Where is *the* library?

根據這種原則，當我們提到地球，月亮這種獨一無二的東西，就必須用"*the*"。

the earth

the sun

the moon

the universe

除此以外，"*the*"還有一個特殊的用途，我們可以在"*the*"的後面加一個形容詞，使這兩個字變成了一個名詞，舉例來說：

the rich＝富人

the poor＝窮人

the weak＝弱者

the deaf＝聾人

the blind＝盲人

請注意，這些名詞是複數：

the rich always get richer.

the poor are getting poorer.

the blind are often very sensitive to sounds.

以下是一些用"*a*"和"*the*"的例子，讀者應設法了解句子中為何有時用"*a*"，有時用"*the*"。

1. He is *a* student.

2. He is *the* student who can swim very well.

3. I like being *a* teacher.

4. He is *the* teacher who taught me English.

5. *The* President of the United States is an important person in the world.

6. I have *a* son and *a* daughter.

7. I have two sons. This is *the* son who will be a doctor.

8. I want to be *a* teacher who is loved by students.

9. He is not *the* person whom we talked about.

10. There is *a* boat in *the* river.

11. This is *the* boat which we used.

12. *The* rain is going to stop tomorrow.

13. We *need* a good rain.

14. *The* weather is really bad.

15. Is there *a* train station near us?

16. Where is *the* station?

17. Do you know where *the* post office is?

18. There is *a* post office inside that building.

19. *The* library looks so good.

20. *The* rich should pay more taxes.

21. We should pay more attention to *the* poor.

22. *The* blind can also study computer science now.

23. *The* earth is round.

24. *The* sun never sets on *the* British Empire.

25. Do you think we can reach *the* moon?

26. How large is *the* universe?

練習五十六

將下列中文句子譯成英文：

1.他是一個好學生。

2.他是那位老師都喜歡的學生。

3.我要做總統。

4.這是總統。

5.請打開一扇窗。

6.中華民國的總統將於明年訪問美國。

7.我要做一個好的工程師。

8.他是那位我們常常談到的老師。

9.Java是一個新的計算機語言。

10.我有一隻狗。

11.他是那位獲大獎的教授。

12.火車站在哪裡？

13.請告訴我郵局的地址。

14.這裡有郵局嗎？

15.太陽在東邊升起。

16.宇宙是非常大的。

17.為什麼我們白天不能看到月亮？

18.總統幾歲？

練習五十七

將適當的冠詞填入下列的空白：

1. He is _____ student who went to see you.

2. There is _____ river in this area.

3. I don't want to be _____ teacher.

4. He wants to become _____ doctor.

5. No one wants to be _____ beggar.

6. Please open _____ door which opens to the hall.

7. UNIX is _____ computer operating system.

8. WINDOWS is _____ only operating system invested in by Microsoft.

9. I have _____ dog and two cats.

10. Is she _____ teacher whom we talked about yesterday?

11. _____ earth is not flat.

12. Is there _____ hotel around here?

13. Where is _____ train station?

14. I really like _____ library.

15. Please give me _____ glass of water.

16. _____ wind is getting stronger and stronger.

17. He is _____ friend of mine.

18. It is hard for _____ poor to go to college.

19. He is _____ swimmer who swam across the English Channel.

20. _____ weather is getting colder and colder.

21. This is _____ book which I bought yesterday.

22. I don't want to be _____ professor.

23. I am going to take _____ vacation next month.

24. John will become _____ basketball player.

25. I ride _____ bicycle to work every morning.

12.2 a和an的用法

在英文裡，"a"有時必須用"an"代替，凡是一個字一開始的發音是母音的話，那麼前面就不能用"a"，而必須用"an"。例子：

an apple

an answer

an egg

an eye

an island

an idea

an old lady

an odd case

an umbrella

請注意，用"an"與否並不是完全和字母有關，而是和發音有關。舉例來說，"*u*"雖然是一個母音字母，但是我們卻說"*a unit*"，而不能用*"*an unit*"，因為"*unit*"的一開始發音並非母音。

其他類似的例子有：

a useful car

a university

a uniform

a one-sided opinion

　　反過來說，有些字並不以母音開始，但是卻必須用"an"，因為這些字的第一音節是母音發音，例子：

　　an honest person
　　an hour

練習五十八

填入"a"或"an"：

1. He is _____ English Professor.

2. This is _____ easy job.

3. He is just _____ ordinary person.

4. _____ friend in need is _____ friend indeed.

5. Give me _____ hint.

6. I have _____ American friend.

7. I will become _____ engineer.

8. Is he _____ honest boy?

9. _____ hour later, he went away.

10. Where is _____ university library?

11. Is there _____ university library here?

12.3 冠詞使用時的例外

在以上的兩節，我們好像說冠詞的使用是有一定規則的，其實不然，例外也不少。在很多情形之下，冠詞是要省略的，更麻煩的是，連省略冠詞的規則都有例外，應該省的卻又不省了。

第一個有關冠詞的特殊用法是這樣的，假設我們要說「男生通常不喜歡彈鋼琴」，我們不能說：

Boy does not like to play the piano.

而要說：

Boys do not like to play the piano.

這時，"*boys*"的前面，是沒有冠詞的，理由很簡單，我們不能加"*a*"，因為"*boys*"是複數，我們也不能加"*the*"。類似的例子有：

1. *Girls* are more diligent than boys.

2. When spring comes, *flowers* start to bloom.

3. *Dogs* are often close to their masters.

4. *Cats* are often quite lazy.

5. *Men* eat more than women.

6. *Professors* are all very smart.

第二個規則有關所謂不可數名詞，很多名詞是可以數的，如：

a cup, two cups

a boy, three boys

a teacher

a student

a boat

an airplane

a glass of water

a cup of tea

可是很多名詞在抽象的狀況下，是不可數的，如：

time, love, hatred, pain, joy, sadness, kindness, wisdom, hope, patience

在這種情況之下，這些名詞的前面是不要加冠詞的，例子如下：

1. *Time* flies.（時間過得很快。）

2. We can not live without *love*.

3. Let there be no *hatred*.

4. We must be able to endure *pain*.

5. Loving others creates *joy*.

6. There is sadness in his *voice*.

7. Can you feel his *kindness*?

8. He has *wisdom*.

9. There is *hope* among us.

10. I am losing *patience.*

以上的例子，乃是泛指的事物，如果特定的抽象名詞，仍要加冠詞。例如：

1. This is *the* time to cry.

2. Do you feel *the* pain?

3. Everyone can feel *the* joy of being loved.

4. We just can not avoid *the* sadness of losing some loved ones.

5. He does have *the* patience to listen to long talks.

6. It is *a* virtue not to steal.

以下這些名詞，是物質名詞：

water, fire, air, metal, tea, coffee, bread, butter

如果這些物質名詞泛指一般的東西，前面是不要加冠詞的，例如：

1. Drinking *water* is important.

2. Don't play with *fire.*

3. We need *air* to breathe.

4. There is *metal* in this device.

5. I don't drink *tea.*

6. I like *coffee.*

一旦物質名詞指特定的東西，前面就要加冠詞，例如：

1. *The* water in this city is polluted.

2. There was *a* fire near our home last night.

3. *The* air in this town is getting worse and worse.

4. Copper is *a* metal.

5. *The* tea that I gave him was from India.

專有名詞，一般說來都不要加冠詞的：

1. *Mary* is from Canada.

2. *John* got married last month.

3. *Taiwan* is an island.

4. *England* is in Europe.

5. *France* is a nice country to visit.

6. *Russia* is a large country.

7. *Park Street* is the main street in this city.

8. Go to *Taipei* first.

9. *Sun Moon Lake* is a beautiful lake.

10. *January* is often very cold here.

11. *Sunday* is a day for resting.

12. *Spring* is the best season.

13. *Mt. Everest* is in Asia.

14. *President Kennedy* died when he was young.

15. *King George* was considered a mad king.

16. *Queen Elizabeth* visited Australia recently.

可惜的是，英文中專有名詞仍有要加"*the*"的，我們將試著將這些例外寫成規則，但這種規則一定掛一漏萬，讀者如要知道何種情況要加冠詞，何種情況不加冠詞，惟一的辦法是多讀英文的文章，慢慢地就會了解什麼情形該用冠詞，什麼情形不用冠詞。

哪些專門名詞前面仍要加冠詞"*the*"呢？

（1）河流、海洋、沙漠、海峽海灣等等專有名詞的前面都要加
　　 "*the*"。

> the Hudson River（赫德森河）
>
> the Rhine River（萊茵河）
>
> the Yellow River（黃河）
>
> the River Thames（泰晤士河）
>
> the Amazon River（亞馬遜河）
>
> the Pacific Ocean（太平洋）
>
> the Red Sea（紅海）
>
> the Mediterranean Sea（地中海）
>
> the Baltic Sea（波羅的海）
>
> the Atlantic Ocean（大西洋）
>
> the Sahara Desert（撒哈拉大沙漠）
>
> the Gobi Desert（戈壁大沙漠）
>
> the Taiwan Strait（台灣海峽）
>
> the English Channel（英吉利海峽）
>
> the Manila Bay（馬尼拉海灣）

the Bay of Tokyo（東京灣）

the Persian Gulf（波斯灣）

（2）國家的名詞中如有"*of*"時，要加"*the*"

the United States of America

the Union of Soviet Socialist Republics

the Republic of China

（3）非常正式的名稱，也要加"*the*"

the World Bank（世界銀行）

the United Nations（聯合國）

the Red Cross（紅十字會）

the Catholic Church（天主教會）

（4）帝國、朝代、時代等等專有名詞的前面，要加"*the*"

the British Empire（大英帝國）

the Ottoman Empire（奧圖門帝國）

the United Kingdom（聯合王國）

the Byzantine Era（拜占庭時代）

the Chin Dynasty（秦朝）

the Victorian Period（維多利亞時代）

the Hanover Dynasty（漢諾威王朝）

The Renaissance Era（文藝復興時代）

the Dark Ages（黑暗時代）

（5）如果提到「全體」，就要加 *"the"*

the Wangs（王家）

the Kennedys（甘迺迪家族）

請注意，*"Wang"*和*"Kennedy"*都是姓，如果要指全家人，必須在姓氏的後面加*"s"*，前面加*"the"*。如果指王家的房子，就說*"the Wang's house"*.

the Chinese（中國人）

the Americans（美國人）

the Africans（非洲人）

其他不加冠詞的名詞，以下是一些規則：

（1）學科一概不加冠詞

I do not like *mathematics*.

He hates *geometry*.

She teaches us *history*.

（2）三餐一概不加冠詞

Did you have *lunch.*

Missing *breakfast* is bad for your health.

We have had *dinner* already.

　但是千萬記住，如果我們的名詞指定某一個特定的時候，就仍要加冠詞，以下是一些例子：

1. I had *a* happy Christmas lunch with my family.
2. *The* dinner you treated me with last night was really good.
3. Did you have *a* big breakfast?

（3）假如我們說「上學」，「去教堂」等等，都不要加冠詞，例如：

1. I went to *church* yesterday.
2. He goes to *church* every Sunday.
3. She is going to *college* this summer.
4. Did you go to *school* last week?

　但是如果我們說的是指定的教堂，學校等等，仍要加冠詞，例如：

1. I went to *the* church on the corner of Park Street and Seventh Avenue yesterday.
2. *The* church which I went to when I was young is still there.

3. I did not go to *the* college which my father went to.

（4）語言不要加冠詞

1. *English* is easy to learn.

2. There are also grammatical rules in *Chinese*.

3. Can you speak *Japanese*?

但是，我們必須注意語言有另一種表示的方法，例如：

1. *The* English language is easy to learn.

2. There are grammatical rules in *the* Chinese language.

在以上的句子，"*English*"和"*Chinese*"都是形容詞，不是名詞。

（5）運動一概前面不加冠詞

1. Do you play *tennis*?

2. I can not play *basketball*.

3. I really love *soccer*.

（6）動名詞前面不加冠詞

1. *Swimming* is good for you.

2. I like *playing* tennis.

3. Do you enjoy *playing* piano?

練習五十九

以下的句子都有冠詞用法的錯誤，請改正這些錯誤：

1. The girls are usually good at learning languages.

2. The dogs always chase the cats.

3. I have not had a water for two hours.

4. There is no life without the pain.

5. The love is the most important thing in one's life.

6. He has the wisdom.

7. I am losing the patience.

8. This is not time to cry.

9. Pain due to losing a loved one is hard to endure.

10. Joy of being a father is really great.

11. Being honest is virtue.

12. We need the air to live.

13. I do not drink the coffee. I drink the tea.

14. We Chinese eat the rice every day.

15. Water in this area is very clean.

16. There was fire in the next street last night.

17. Fire last night killed three kids.

18. Coffee which you are drinking is from South America.

19. Mary is from the Canada.

20. The China is a large country.

21. Republic of China was founded in 1911.

22. Where is the England?

23. Is the Russia in Europe?

24. The President Lincoln was a great person.

25. The King George was a mad king.

26. Yellow River is a long river.

27. Have you been to Gobi Desert?

28. Manila Bay is very beautiful.

29. It is hard to cross Atlantic Ocean by a small boat.

30. Can you swim across English Channel?

31. United States of America is a large country.

32. United Nations and Red Cross often work together.

33. When did Ottoman Empire end?

34. British Empire was large before.

35. Catholic Church is one of the oldest organizations in the world.

36. This cup was made in Ming Dynasty.

37. European Renaissance was a very important era for mankind.

38. We should not go back to Dark Ages.

39. Wangs did not invite me to their house.

40. I do not like Kennedys.

41. Chinese pay great attention to education.

42. I do not like the physics.

43. Are you interested in the chemistry?

44. Did you have the lunch?

45. Let us have the dinner together.

46. I always have a breakfast with my family.

47. I had big dinner last night.

48. Dinner my mother cooked for me was delicious.

49. I go to the church every Sunday.

50. He does not like to go to the school.

51. Did you see beautiful church in the next street?

52. The English is so hard for me.

53. Do you speak the English?

54. Do you play the tennis?

55. The swimming is good for you.

練習六十

在以下的空白處加入冠詞，如不需要冠詞，就讓它空白：

1. _____ boys usually do not like to sit still for long.

2. I would love to have _____ cup of coffee.

3. There is _____ love between us.

4. Can you feel _____ love of your mother?

5. _____ joy of having a new baby is really great.

6. We can not live without _____ love.

7. I have not drunk _____ wine for a long time.

8. Do you have _____ wisdom to distinguish bad persons from good ones?

9. This is _____ good dinner.

10. I did not have _____ dinner.

11. _____ joy of being _____ mother is great.

12. _____ running is _____ good exercise.

13. _____ sadness due to the death of his mother really hurts him.

14. We need _____ water to live.

15. We can not live without _____ air.

16. I do not drink _____ coffee.

17. _____fire that occurred last night destroyed my house.

18. _____ coffee which you are drinking is very light.

19. _____ Republic of China is in Asia.

20. Where is _____ Russia?

21. Is _____ France in Africa?

22. _____ President Kennedy was liked by most Americans

before be died.

23. _____ Amazon River is a long one.

24. Have you ever been to _____ Tokyo?

25. Have you ever been to _____ Tokyo Bay?

26. There are more than one hundred countries in _____

United Nations.

27. This is _____ Ming Dynasty porcelain.

28. _____ Wangs invited us to a dinner party.

29. I do not like _____ mathematics.

30. _____ spring is a pleasant season.

31. I had _____ pleasant evening with my friends.

32. _____ breakfast which I had this morning was too light for
    me.

33. It is not easy to study _____ English.

34. I did play _____ basketball yesterday.

35. _____ swimming is _____ good exercise.

36. There should be _____ chicken in every pot.

練習六十一

將以下的句子譯成英文：

1.狗會叫(bark)。

2.貓會抓老鼠。

3.有時候(sometimes)，痛苦是好的。

4.我不喝茶。

5.感覺到被愛是很重要的。

6.說實話令人快樂。

7.我們需要愛。

8.他是一個中國人。

9.中國人喜歡喝茶。

10.昨夜，城裡有一場火。

11.約翰來自美國。

12.法國在哪裡？

13.我喜歡林肯總統。

14.黃河不是黃的。

15.紅十字會已經有一百年了（one hundred years old）。

16.明朝是一個重要的朝代。

17.你喜愛數學嗎？

18.我今天早上沒有吃早飯。

19.我已吃過午飯。

20.我昨天沒有去教堂。

21.我今年秋天要上大學。

22.游泳使我強壯。

第十三章
形容詞的比較級

如果我們要翻譯「他比較老」，我們不能說：

　　* He is more old.

而一定要說：

　　He is older.

為什麼呢？這是因為英文裡面的形容詞有所謂的比較級規則。在下一節，我們講一些最基本的規則。

 ## 13.1 最基本的規則

首先，我們要說明英文形容詞有三個等級：原級、比較級和最高級，最基本的規則是根據音節的多少來分的。一般來說，單音節的形容詞在字後面加 *"er"*，就變成了比較級，加 *"est"* 就變成了最高級，而通常雙音節，或雙音節以上的形容詞，比較級是在字前面加 *"more"*，最高級則是在字前面加 *"most"*，舉例來說，*"old"*， "*smart*", "*strong*", "*weak*", "*high*", "*low*"等等都是單音節的形容詞，他們的變化如下：

原級	比較級	最高級
old	older	oldest
smart	smarter	smartest
strong	stronger	strongest
weak	weaker	weakest
high	higher	highest
low	lower	lowest

以上的形容詞，都是單音節的，以下的例子都有關雙音節的形容詞：

原級	比較級	最高級
difficult	more difficult	most difficult
delicious	more delicious	most delicious
beautiful	more beautiful	most beautiful
correct	more correct	most correct
stupid	more stupid	most stupid
significant	more significant	most significant

有一個規則必須注意，我們不能將"*more*"和"*er*"混在一齊用，以下的例子都是錯的：

＊He is more older than I.

＊He is more taller than his brother.

正確的句子是：

He is older than I.

He is taller than his brother.

練習六十二

寫出以下形容詞的比較級：

1. small

2. slow

3. intelligent

4. expensive

5. tall

6. short

7. important

8. cheap

9. famous

10. cold

11. fast

12. careful

13. colorful

14. long

15. dark

16. bright

13.2 特殊的比較級規則

在上一節，我們說明了最基本的規則，那就是單音節形容詞加"*er*"或"*est*"，雙音節的形容詞前面加"*more*"或 "*most*"。但以下就是這些基本規則的例外。

（1）單音節形容詞的字是"*e*"，就直接加"*r*"或"*st*"

原級	比較級	最高級
large	larger	largest
late	later	latest
nice	nicer	nicest
wise	wiser	wisest

（2）形容詞的字尾是*y*，而前一個子母是一個子音，則除掉*y*，加上"*ier*"，或"*iest*"：

原級	比較級	最高級
lucky	luckier	luckiest
happy	happier	happiest
pretty	prettier	prettiest
dry	drier	driest
easy	easier	easiest

（3）單音節形容詞的字尾是子音，前一音是一個母音，則字尾必須重複一次，再加"*er*"或"*est*"

原級	比較級	最高級
fat	fatter	fattest
hot	hotter	hottest
wet	wetter	wettest
big	bigger	biggest

（4）完全不規則的變化：

英文中，有幾個特殊的字，他們的比較級完全沒有規則，以下是一些例子，讀者必須記住。

原級	比較級	最高級
good well	better	best
bad	worse	worst
many much	more	most

練習六十三

寫下以下形容詞的比較級：

1. cute

2. wide

3. early

4. happy

5. heavy

6. thin

7. easy

8. hot

9. wise

10. large

11. good

12. bad

13. many

13.3 比較級的用法

大多數比較級句子裡會有"*than*"，以下是一些例子：

1. I am older than he.

2. His English is better than mine.

3. San Francisco is more beautiful than New York.

4. His car is cheaper than your car.

5. He is the most diligent student in his class.

6. I like apples more than I like oranges.

7. He has more money than his brother.

8. He is stronger than his brother.

必須注意的是以下的句子是錯的：

    *I am older than him.

    *She is smarter than me.

為什麼錯了呢？因為原來句子應該是：

    I am older than he (is).

    She is smarter than I (am).

習慣上的"*is*"和"*am*"都省略掉的，由以上的解釋可以看出，"*than*"後面的句詞應該是主詞，而非受詞。

以下的錯誤，也請特別注意：

　　*My head is larger than your.

正確的句子是：

　　My head is larger than your head.

或者　My head is larger than yours.

請看以下幾個錯誤的句子：

*My house is larger than your.

*The temperature of this city is higher than San Francisco.

*The height of Mt. Everest is greater than Mt. Fuji.

正確的句子應該是：

1. My house is larger than your house.

2. My house is larger than yours.

3. The temperature of this city is higher than the temperature of San Francisco.

4. The temperature of this city is higher than that of San Francisco.

5. The height of Mt. Everest is greater than the height of Mt. Fuji.

6. The height of Mt. Everest is greater than that of Mt. Fuji.

請注意以下的例子，句子中沒有"*than*"，但仍有比較級：

1. Among all the teachers who have taught me, he is the best.

2. This is the best movie I have ever seen.

3. This food is the worst that I have ever eaten.

4. John is the stronger one.

5. Do we have a better choice?

6. Mary is the more diligent one.

7. He is the older of the two.

8. He is one of the best movie actors.

9. This area is one of the hottest areas in the world.

10. He is one of the fastest swimmers in the United States.

11. This is a book which I like the most.

練習六十四

改錯：

1. He is more old than I.

2. She is younger than me.

3. This university is more larger than that university.

4. He is more older than my brother.

5. His house is older than my.

6. The size of this city is larger than San Francisco.

7. She is taller than him.

8. The height of this boy is greater than his brother.

9. He is the most good student in my class.

10. He is the more bad one.

練習六十五

將下列句子譯成英文句子：

1. 你比他強壯。

2. 他的英文比我的好。

3. 他比他的弟弟更富有。

4. 他是世界上最富有的人。

5. 這支筆比你的貴得多。

6. 他是世界上最高的人。

7. 亞馬遜河是世界上最長的河。

8. 他比他的爸爸高。

9. 他是班上最好的學生。

10. 在我遇到的人中，他是最高的。

練習六十六

填充：

1. He is _____ (old) than John.

2. This problem is one of the _____ (difficult) problems that I have ever seen.

3. This is one of the _____ (good) movies that I have ever seen.

4. Do we have a _____ (good) choice?

5. This place is _____ (hot) than San Francisco.

6. He is _____ (famous) than his sister.

7. She is getting _____ (bad) now.

8. He is feeling _____ (well) now.

9. He has _____ (much) money than his father.

10. Mary is one of _____ (beautiful) students in her class.

11. He is _____ (happy) than before.

12. Peter is getting _____ (thin).

13. This summer is _____ (hot) than last summer.

14. You have a _____ (bright) future now.

15. He has _____ (many) students than I.

16. I feel much _____ (well) now.

17. He is _____ (careful) than you.

18. Time is _____ (important) than money.

第十四章
總複習的例子

在這一章，我們將給很多簡短的文章，每一段文章的後面，我們都會有詳細的解釋，相信這些解釋將有助於讀者對於文法的了解。

 （1）

Dear Mother:

I arrived at the Taipei Train Station around one o'clock in the afternoon yesterday. My friend, Mr. Chen, greeted me at the station. We took a taxi to go directly to the university and checked into the dormitory. The dormitory is a very old one. I will live with three other boys, and I met two of them already. Both of them are from Taichung, and they are both quite friendly.

We went to the dormitory cafeteria for dinner. The food is not that good. Dear Mother, I miss you and especially the food you cooked for me.

Your son

這封信很簡單，所敘述的事情不是用簡單的現在式，就是簡單的過去式，當然也有一次用了未來式。

絕大多數的句子都用了簡單的過去式，因為這些句子都是敘述過去所發生的事，用現在式的有以下幾句：

1. The dormitory is a very old one.

2. Both of them are from Taichung.

3. The food is not that good.

4. I miss you and the food you cooked for me.

為什麼這幾句話要用現在式呢？道理很簡單，這幾句話描寫的是一些狀態，而並非過去發生的事。

1. "The dormitory is a very old one."

2. "Both of them are from Taichung."

3. "The food is not that good."

4. "I miss you and the food you cooked for me."

這四個句子都是目前存在的事實，所以要用現在式。

現在我們不妨看一下冠詞的情形，我們可以看到很多地方都用了"the"，如：

the Taipei Train Station

the afternoon

the station

the university

the dormitory cafeteria

the dormitory

the food

the food you cooked for me

各位讀者一定可以注意到在"*the*"後面的名詞都有所指，舉例來說，"*the university*"指那所作者要去唸的大學，他的媽媽知道他所說的是那一所大學。"*The dormitory*"指那間他已搬進去住的宿舍。凡是有所指的名詞前面，原則上都應該加"*the*"。

哪裡用了"*a*"呢？注意，我們用了兩次：

a taxi

a very old one

讀者應該不難看出爲什麼這裡我們不能用"*the*"，而一定要用"*a*"。

 （2）

Mary: "Hello, this is Mary. Who is calling?"

John: "Hi, this is John. How are you?"

Mary: "I am doing fine. In fact, I am studying for the final
　　　examination now."

John: "Oh, I am sorry. When will the exam be over?"

Mary: "This Friday."

John: "Then, can we have dinner Friday evening?"

Mary: "OK, where are we going to eat?"

John: "How about the Chinese restaurant called Four Seasons?"

Mary: "That is all right with me. When do we meet?"

John: "How about six o'clock?"

Mary: "That's fine. See you Friday evening at 6 o'clock at the Four Seasons."

這一篇短文主要的目的在於介紹所謂現在進行式。

1. Who is calling.

2. I am doing fine.

3. I am studying for the final examination now.

都是標準的現在進行式，事實上，也必須用現在進行式。

 （3）

I have been interested in music ever since I was a small child. When I was seven years old, my mother gave me a violin as a birthday present. I have been taking violin lessons ever since.

I was so interested in music that I finally decided to

go to music school. This was a hard decision for me. I consulted with my parents. Both of them encouraged me to go ahead.

　　Yesterday, I was accepted by one of the best music schools in Taiwan.　I am really happy about this.

　　這一段話中，我們開始用現在完成式，比方說第一句話就是：

I have been interested in music ever since I was a small child.

　　為什麼要用現在完成式呢？道理很簡單，這句話裡面有有 "*ever since*" 這個詞，凡是有了這個詞句，我們就一定要用現在完成式了。

　　另外一句用了現在完成進行式的句子是：

I have been taking violin lessons ever since.

　　讀者不妨去看看第四章，就知道為什麼這裡要用現在完成進行式了。凡是「自從」某某日開始，而就一直在做的事情，就應該用現在完成式，或者現在完成進行式。

　　這一段文章裡面，我們還用了被動語氣。

I was accepted by one of the best music schools in Taiwan.

　　各位讀者不妨注意，這被動語氣的用法是很正當而且適宜的，如用主動這句話變成了：

One of the best music schools accepted me.

　　這樣反而並不太能表達原意。

 （4）

　　Before I got into college, I had been to the United States and lived there for one year. This is why I could speak English better than other students in my classes.

　　When I was taking classes in college, Hitler was secretly preparing for the Second World War. The war erupted finally when I was a senior. I was forced to quit school and was drafted into the army. Luckily I survived the war and came back to continue my studies after the war was over. Since I had been in the war, I was more mature than most of the other students.

　　Even now, I can still remember how my days as a college student were different from my days as a soldier.

　　這篇文章介紹了如何使用過去完成式，第一句話就用了過去完成式，因為有兩件事，一件是「進大學」，另一件是「去過美國」，由於在進大學以前去美國，所以去「美國」就用了過去完成式。

　　請注意第二段的第一句：

When I was taking classes in college, Hitler was secretly preparing for the Second World War.

　　這一次，我們用了過去進行式，因為有兩件事，「在學校唸書」是一件事，「希特勒在準備發動第二次世界大戰」是另一件事，其中有一件可以用過去完成式。

　　同理，在第二段話的最後一句話中，「曾經去打過仗」用了過去完成式。

　　這段文章中，有一句話用了被動語氣，讀者不妨看這句話 *I was forced to quit school.*，其實我們在這種情形之下，我們必須用被動語氣，當然也可以用主動語氣，不過那並不太自然。

　　也請讀者注意這段文章的最後一句話仍一定要用現在式。

 （5）

　　I have been interested in reading novels for a long time. Among all of the novels that I have read, I like detective novels the most.Out of all the detective novels, I especially like those written by Agatha Christe.

　　Last year, I started reading another kind of novel, namely science fiction. I found that some science fiction writers are quite philosophical.   Unfortunately, there are not too many of them.

I have always had the dream that one day I will be good at writing novels. Do you think that my dream might come true?

這段文章中，我們介紹了動名詞的用法，第一句話的 "*reading*"就是動名詞，除此以外，我們還有兩處用了動名詞："*started reading*"和"*good at writing*"。

讀者也應該了解爲什麼第一句話要用現在完成進行式，在第二句話裡面，當我們形容"*novels*"，我們也用了現在完成式。

請讀者注意第一段的最後一句話，"those written by Agatha Christe"。在這裡，"written"是一個過去分詞用作了形容詞，形容"novels"，我們也可以說"those which were written by Agatha Christe."

順便講一下，"Agatha Christ e"是一位非常著名的偵探小說作者。

也請大家注意，我們只能說"interested in reading"，而不能說 "interesting in reading"。

 (6)

Tomorrow, there will be a dancing party in our university. Since we are freshmen and most of us have never been to a large dancing party, we are naturally very excited. I must say that I am not that excited. Although dancing is interesting, I often think that the music is too loud.   Besides, as a bystander, I often find the way that the young people dance these days is so funny. When they dance, they often remind me of monkeys.

Well, I must admit that playing basketball is more interesting to me. But, unfortunately, I cannot play basketball tomorrow because the courts will be used for the dancing party.

這一段話主要的目的是介紹現在分詞和過去分詞用成形容詞的做法。第一個現在分詞是"*dancing*","*dancing*"在這裡形容"*party*"。

我們在這裡看到有些時候，我們應該用現在分詞，有時要用過去分詞。請看以下的句子：

We are naturally very much excited.

在這裡，我們一定要用"*excited*"，絕對不能用：

*We are naturally very exciting.

下一句：

Although dancing is interesting,

這裡，我們必須用"*interesting*"，而不能用"*interested*"。也就是說，我們不能說：*Although dancing is interested.

（7）

We probably all believe that we should love others and forgive those who do bad things to us. Unfortunately it is often hard for us to practice what we believe in. For example, if someone really hurts us badly, we just do not know what we should do.　Should we take some kind of action to hurt the person who hurt us, or should we forgive him?

　　　　The truth is that we may still seek justice. It is right if we want a criminal to go to jail for his crime. Yet, we should never have hatred in our hearts.

這篇文章的目的在介紹「子句」的用法，請注意這篇文章內的很多子句，舉例來說：

　　that we should love others and forgive those who do bad
　　things.

就是一個子句，這個子句是*"believe"*的受詞，有趣的是，這個子句內部又有一個子句，那就是：

　　who do bad things to do.
這個子句是形容*"those"*的。

以下是這一段文章的全部子句：

1. that we should love others and forgive those
2. who do bad things to us
3. what we believe in
4. what we should do
5. that we may still seek justice

第十五章

各種文法錯誤列表

　　我們中國人寫英文句子的時侯，總免不了會犯一些錯誤，這一章將這些錯誤列成表，讀者每次寫好一篇文章，不妨先查查看有沒有犯這些錯誤。

　　請注意，凡是有 * 的句子，都是有錯的。越是編號在前面的越容易，凡是犯前面錯誤的讀者，該好好檢討了。

 ERROR 1. 兩個動詞聯在一起用。

*I am love you.

*He wants drink water.

*The Second World War was happened in 1939.

*The world is changes all the time.

*He needs spend a lot of money.

*His mother encourages him work hard.

*Many people were died during the war.

*I asked him come back.

*Many people were gave up.

*He seems doesn't care.

正確的句子是：

I love you.

He wants to drink water.

The Second World War happened in 1939.

The world changes all the time.

He needs to spend a lot of money.

His mother encourages him to work hard.

Many people died during the war.

I asked him to come back.

Many people gave up.

He doesn't seem to care.

ERROR 2. 單數第三人稱現在式，動詞忘了加 s.

*He like you.

*My uncle go to work by bus.

*I don't know what the government do to stimulate the economy.

正確的句子是：

He likes you.

My uncle goes to work by bus.

I don't know what the government does to stimulate the economy.

ERROR 3. 忘了有些助動詞後面一定要用原形動詞。

*He did not went to school yesterday.

*He will not goes to church.

*He does not likes you.

*I should not gave him the book.

*He does not enjoying the conversation.

正確的句子是：

He did not go to school yesterday.

He will not go to church.

He does not like you.

I should not give him the book.

He does not enjoy the conversation.

ERROR 4. 忘了在 to 的後面一定要用原形動詞。

*I like to swimming.

*I forgot to went to school.

正確的句子是：

I like to swim.

I forgot to go to school.

ERROR 5. 動詞和主詞不一致。

*I were at home last night.

*He have no money to buy that book.

*They was good friends.

*His ability to accomplish many things at the same time are great.

*Their wishes was finally realized.

正確的句子是：

I was at home last night.

He has no money to buy that book.

They were good friends.

His ability to accomplish many things at the same time is great.

Their wishes were finally realized.

ERROR 6. 句子沒有動詞。

*He looking for a book.

*Many people interested in music.

*He very happy.

*That car having many passengers in it.

*The President towards the people.

*The future good for us.

*Many banks bankrupt.

*It may due to the war.

正確的句子是：

He is looking for a book.

Many people are interested in music.

He is very happy.

That car has many passengers in it.

The President walked towards the people.

The future is good for us

Many banks are bankrupt.

It may be due to the war.

ERROR 7. 句子沒有主詞。

*How can protect human beings?

*This way, at least don't kill people.

正確的句子是：

How can we protect human beings?

This way, at least we don't kill people.

ERROR 8. 動詞的時態錯了。

*He watches TV now.

*The earth was round.

*Two points defined a line.

*She sings a song now.

*Hitler kills millions of Jewish people during the Second World War.

*When I went to see him yesterday, he is watching TV.

*He lived here since he was ten years old.

*He lived here since 1980.

*When the President visits the village last week, people are joyful to see him.

*He has lived here since he had been a child.

*Many industries leave this country.

正確的句子是：

He is watching TV now.

The earth is round.

Two points define a line.

She is singing a song now.

Hitler killed millions of Jewish people during the Second World War.

When I went to see him yesterday, he was watching TV.

He has lived here since he was ten years old.

He has lived here since 1980.

When the President visited the village last week, people were joyful to see him.

He has lived here since he was a child.

Many industries are leaving this country

ERROR 9. 忘了在 verb to have 的後面應該用過去分詞。

*He has wrote a novel.

*I have finish the report.

正確的句子是：

He has written a novel.

I have finished the report.

ERROR 10. 在被動語氣 verb to be 的後面忘了用過去分詞。

*He is like by every one.

*Rice is grow in this country.

正確的句子是：

He is liked by every one.

Rice is grown in this country.

ERROR 11. 動詞用成了名詞。

*I like play tennis.

*Kill people cannot solve the problem.

*We should put more effort into write English compositions.

正確的句子是：

I like to play tennis.

Killing people cannot solve the problem.

We should put more effort into writing English compositions.

ERROR 12. 動詞用成了形容詞。

*This is a win team.

*He is a cry baby.

正確的句子是：

This is a winning team.

He is a crying baby.

ERROR 13. 該有助動詞的句子沒有助動詞。

*Why he killed him?

*Why they came so late?

正確的句子是：

Why did he kill him?

Why did they come so late?

ERROR 14. 該用被動語氣的地方用了主動語氣。

*He transformed into a good person.

*Wine manufactured in this country.

*The books will be shipping to you.

*This is a book writing by Professor Smith.

*A network has been establishing.

正確的句子是：

He was transformed into a good person.

Wine is manufactured in this country.

The books will be shipped to you.

This is a book written by Professor Smith.

A network has been established.

ERROR 15. 兩個句子中間忘了用 "when"、 "where"、"who" ...等。

*He is a man can run very fast.

*I am a person swims every morning.

*There are more people help themselves.

*Those students live far away can live in our dormitory.

*There are 8 million people use mobile phones.

正確的句子是：

He is a man who can run very fast.

I am a person who swims every morning.

There are more people who help themselves.

Those students who live far away can live in our dormitory.

There are 8 million people who use mobile phones.

以上的句子有些也可以以下的形式出現：

He is a man able to run very fast.

There are more people helping themselves.

Those students living far away can live in our dormitory.

There are 8 million people using mobile phones.

ERROR 16. 忘了在 "which"、"that" ... 後面應該用子句，而非片語。

*Products which consuming a lot of energy are not good for us.

*We should not leave before the concert ending.

*We will lose when other countries having better technologies.

*We cannot win if lacking courage.

*There is a company, which called Value America.

*This is a group of people which made up of lawyers.

*We often use appliances which made in Japan.

正確的句子是：

Products which consume a lot of energy are not good for us.

We should not leave before the concert ends.

We will lose when other countries have better technologies.

We cannot win if we lack courage.

There is a company which is called Value America.

This is a group of people which is made up of lawyers.

We often use appliances which are made in Japan.

ERROR 17. 不該用 "to" 的地方用了 "to"。

*I will not let you to cry.

*He made wars to disappear.

*I heard him to laugh.

*I made my son to wash my car.

正確的句子是：

I will not let you cry.

He made wars disappear.

I heard him laugh.

I made my son wash my car.

ERROR 18. 忘了有些動詞必須以分詞形式出現。

*He will interest in music when he grows up.

*I disappoint that you did not show up

*He confuses about the story.

*Tom excites by the good news.

*I satisfy with your work.

正確的句子是：

He will be interested in music when he grows up.

I am disappointed that you did not show up.

He is confused about the story.

Tom is excited by the good news

I am satisfied with your work.

ERROR 19. 過去分詞和現在分詞用反了。.

*He is interesting in music.

*He is exciting about the book.

*Sorry, I am confusing about what you said.

*I am greatly disappointing by what you said.

*I was greatly disturbing by his presence.

*This news is interested to me.

*The story is confused to everyone.

*This music is excited to young kids.

*His work is satisfied.

正確的句子是：

He is interested in music.

He is excited about the book.

Sorry, I am confused about what you said.

I am greatly disappointed by what you said.

I was greatly disturbed by his presence.

This news is interesting to me.

The story is confusing to everyone.

This music is exciting to young kids.

His work is satisfying.

ERROR 20. 不及物動詞以被動語氣出現。

*Your paper will be appeared soon.

*He will be disappeared.

*The war will be happened soon.

*Wars were occurred many times in China.

正確的句子是：

Your paper will appear soon.

He will disappear.

The war will happen soon.

Wars occurred many times in China.

ERROR 21. 形容詞用作了名詞。

*I cannot live in poor.

*This cannot eliminate the possible of wars.

正確的句子是：

I cannot live in poverty.

This cannot eliminate the possibility of wars.

ERROR 22. 不該用疑問句的子句用了疑問句。

*I do not know why did he come here.

*No one knows what is Peter doing these days.

正確的句子是：

I do not know why he came here.

No one knows what Peter is doing these days.

練習六十七

改正以下句子的錯誤。

1. Many people like drink wine.

2. He is loves you.

3. He wants go to school.

4. Do you like swim?

5. I told him come back soon.

6. I asked my brother eat an apple every day.

7. My school classmates likes to get together.

8. My government wish to establish a peaceful society.

9. Tom never work hard.

10. He does not telling the truth.

11. I will not going to the concert.

12. I liked to swam.

13. It is important to going to church every Sunday.

14. I were with my brother when you called.

15. My friends is friendly to me.

16. The governments of Asia has no choice

17. His wish to succeed in many things are not realistic.

18. My wish to visit many countries are finally fulfilled.

19. I am a person who eat an apple every day.

20. He not a good student.

21. Many people excited by the news.

22. The future bright.

23. This caused by the war.

24. How can obtain lasting peace?

25. How can succeed?

26. Good citizens are loving their country.

27. I am never watching TV.

28. He had published many books since 1989.

29. I have lived here since I have been ten years old.

30. He is in the university when the war broke out.

31. Many Jewish people are killed during the Second World War.

32. I was a Catholic since 1939.

33. Many people leaving that country because of the poverty.

34. He is writing a letter when I visited him yesterday.

35. He is happy when he was informed of the good news.

36. He has write many novels.

37. I have finally finish the letter.

38. He is not love by anyone.

39. Wine is manufacture here.

40. His effort is well appreciate.

41. I like play basketball.

42. We should pay attention to write good English sentences.

43. Instead of play guitar, he plays violin.

44. This is a lose team.

45. He has a smile face.

46. Why he cried so loudly?

47. He likes not his brother.

48. He not speaks English.

49. Among all of your students, whom you like most?

50. He loved by everyone.

51. This problem transformed into another problem.

52. This line connects to the central office.

53. The books will be mailing to you.

54. He is the man stole my car.

55. Peter is the boy runs very fast.

56. I did not know the war broke out so soon.

57. The boys study hard will easily succeed.

58. There are a lot of people use computers now.

59. I will let you to drive my new car.

60. He makes everyone to laugh.

61. I heard him to sing.

62. He is making his son to go abroad.

63. I will never let him can cheat.

64. His mother makes him must get up early in the morning.

65. He is exciting about the news.

66. He is not interesting in sports.

67. This is not interested to me.

68. His work is well appreciating by all of us.

69. I am disappointing.

70. President Lee will be appeared soon.

71. It will never be happened.

72. He is the most frustrating person.

73. He is living in poor.

74. There is no possible of war.

75. Everyone knows who is he.

76. Do you know why is he so happy?

77. It is hard to explain why did John fail.

78. He is the most cleverest person on earth.

79. Is he getting more and more big?

80. This is the more taller building.

解答

【練習一】

1. I love my parents.
2. He loves his teacher.
3. He keeps swimming every day.
4. He wants to drink a glass of water.
5. He likes playing the violin.
6. Jack does not like mathematics.
7. Mary hates singing.
8. My mother cooks very good food.
9. He wants me to see him tomorrow.
10. He does not know my name.
11. I do not like you.
12. He does not like swimming.
13. You did not go home.
14. I do not like swimming.
15. I wanted to go to my mother's home.
16. I do not like swimming.
17. I did not eat dinner.

18. I will not go home.

19. He did not go home.

20. You may leave now.

21. He can swim.

22. He does not go to work.

【練習二】

1. He is a good student.

2. My elder brother is seventeen years old.

3. My younger brother swims every day.

4. All of them like music.

5. They are in Japan now.

6. Jade Mountain is a very high mountain.

7. The Amazon River is a long river.

8. His father is a teacher.

9. All of us like Chinese food.

10. He doesn't like ice cream.

11. I love you.

12. Everyone is afraid of snakes.

13. Everyone likes dogs.

14. It is very cold today.

【練習三】

1. He is watching a movie.

2. I am swimming.

3. She is making a phone call to her mother.

4. His brother is taking a walk.

5. I am eating now.

6. We are singing.

7. He is playing the piano.

8. He is reading a novel.

9. I am writing a letter.

10. He is running.

【練習四】

1. I love you.

2. I am eating dinner/lunch now.

3. He is not a student.

4. I am a teacher.

5. I am singing.

6. He is swimming now.

7. He likes swimming.

8. He can sing.

9. He is singing now.

10. His father is a doctor.

11. His father is in the U. S. A.

12. I am taking a bath.

13. He is sleeping now.

14. Your sister is riding her bicycle now.

15. Your sister goes to school by bicycle.

【練習五】

1. I attended a party yesterday.

2. His elder brother called me yesterday.

3. I went to America last year.

4. I met your sister last night.

5. I wrote a letter to you.

6. I ate an egg this morning.

7. Last night, he danced all night.

8. We ran five thousand meters yesterday.

9. He was very tired last night.

10. He visited his father in Taipei last night.

【練習六】

1. He is a strong boy.

2. He was sick yesterday.

3. He eats an apple every day.

4. He ate three apples yesterday.

5. I like to watch movies.

6. I am a happy man.

7. I watched two movies yesterday.

8. He sent a letter to you yesterday.

9. He smokes very often.

10. I read the Bible every day.

11. He did not read the Bible yesterday.

12. He did not swim yesterday.

【練習七】

1. He is playing basketball now.

2. He likes playing basketball.

3. He played basketball yesterday.

4. He goes to school by bicycle every day.

5. He went to the country by bicycle yesterday.

6. I like singing.

7. He is singing now.

8. Your father came to see me yesterday.

9. His older brother walks two kilometers every day.

10. His younger brother is a good boy.

11. He was very weak last year.

12. He is making a phone call now.

13. He works hard every day.

14. Your younger brother likes swimming.

15. He was a good student before.

【練習八】

1. It was raining when he went to school yesterday.

2. He was reading a newspaper when the train stopped.

3. They were singing when the train arrived in the station.

4. He was talking to his father on the phone when I arrived at his house yesterday.

5. I was watching TV at home when the clock struck eight last night.

6. I was brushing my teeth when my father called me on the phone last night.

7. He was swimming when I called him.

8. That dog was sleeping when the cat came in.

9. He was playing the violin when his younger brother came home.

10. My mother was cooking dinner when my father came home.

【練習九】

1. I am a Christian.

2. He was a Catholic when he was a child.

3. I went to see my mother yesterday.

4. I like to play the piano.

5. He is eating now.

6. He likes to eat ice cream.

7. He walks to school every day.

8. He is walking now.

9. He is a good boy.

10. He was swimming when I called him.

11. He _went_ to see his mother yesterday.

12. I _was taking_ a bath when my mother called me.

13. I _like_ to swim.

14. I _liked_ to swim when I was young. Now, I don't because I am too old.

15. It _is raining_ now.

16. It _was raining_ when I drove to work yesterday.

17. It _rained_ last night.

18. It _rains_ very often here.

19. He _was reading_ a book when I went to see him yesterday.

20. I _was_ a student when I was young. Now I am a teacher.

【練習十】

1. They were driving when I went to see them yesterday.

2. It rains very often in Taipei.

3. He gave his book to his brother last month.

4. He goes to work every morning.

5. He likes to tell stories.

6. I like to go to church.

7. The sun is setting now.

8. They are playing the piano now.

9. I love you.

10. He was a good student before.

11. He went to church last Sunday.

12. It rained last night.

13. I was playing when you called.

14. It was raining when I drove to work last night.

15. He does not know me.

16. I was swimming when my mother came.

17. They are singing now.

18. He does not like to swim.

19. He always wears a black coat.

20. He is watching TV now.

【練習十一】

1. I have swum every morning since 1980.

2. I have received your letter.

3. I have never been to America.

4. He has been a Christian since he was a child.

5. I have seen your grandfather.

6. Your brother has always lived here.

7. He has learned to play the piano for a long time.

8. I have already written three letters, but he didn't reply.

9. For the past three years, I have driven this car.

10. He has been a teacher since 1975.

11. He has taught English for a long time.

12. I have seen *Gone with the Wind.*

13. I have eaten.

14. I have been to the beach three times this year.

15. I have loved you all my life.

【練習十二】

1. I went to see *Gone with the Wind* yesterday.

2. I have never seen *Gone with the Wind.*

3. I lived in America last year.

4. I have lived in America since 1985.

5. He has never been to England.

6. He has finished the report.

7. I finished the report last night.

8. I saw your father last night.

9. I have seen your father so many times already.

10. I have lived in Tai-Chung all my life.

【練習十三】

1. I _had become_ a Christian already when I was a child.

2. I _have been_ a Christian all my life.

3. He _has lived_ here since 1939.

4. Stop eating now. You _have eaten_ too much.

5. It _rained_ last night.

6. John is a writer. He _has written_ thirteen novels.

7. Last night, I __saw__ your father for the first time in my life.

8. I __talked__ to my father last night.

9. Since 1961, I __have been__ a teacher.   Before that, I <u>was</u> a student.

10. I __have read__ many novels written by Charles Dickens.

【練習十四】

1. We have been working hard since we were little kids.

2. Since last year, he has been studying English.

3. It has been raining since yesterday.

4. Since five o'clock, he has been doing his homework.

5. I have been living in Taichung since I was three years old.

【練習十五】

1. I had met your mother before I was fourteen years old.

2. I had been to America before 1974.

3. He read the Bible six years ago.

4. I had been an engineer before I studied in the university.

5. I had called you before you came.

6. I had met Mr. Lee before I had dinner with him last night.

7. He had been a good president before he resigned.

8. He had been a good doctor before he died.

9. He had been practicing singing before he started going to the

church.

10. It had been raining before eight o'clock this morning.

【練習十六】

1. You were singing when he went to see you yesterday.

2. He had been a good boy.

3. All of them like to play basketball.

4. We are watching TV now.

5. You have lived in Taiwan for a long time.

6. I have already read over this book.

7. They have lived here all the time.

8. I had gone to church before coming here.

9. He likes to watch the sunrise.

10. He likes swimming.

11. He has been learning to play the piano since he was six years old.

12. He used to be a strong boy.

13. He had been a very healthy man before he got sick.

14. People were dancing when the train arrived at the station.

15. He had been a musician before the war broke out.

16. I have seen you before.

17. I saw you last year.

18. I have already written the letter.

19. Since 1974, I have been a soldier.

20. I have read many English books.

【練習十七】

1. He _loves_ his country.

2. He _loved_ his country, but now he does not.

3. I _have been_ a teacher since 1975.

4. I _had been_ a teacher before I went to college.

5. I _have been reading_ Shakespeare ever since I was a little girl.

6. When I went to see her yesterday, she _was watching_ TV.

7. I _had seen_ your father before I saw you.

8. He _has read_ many detective stories.

9. He _goes_ to church every Sunday.

10. It _was_ a cold day yesterday.

11. It _has been raining_ for the last two days.

12. I _have eaten_ too much. I am full now.

13. She _had been_ a nurse before the war broke out.

14. I _have_ never _seen_ you in my life.

15. He _has been_ a teacher since 1980.

16. It _is_ good to eat vegetables every day.

17. It _was_ so nice to meet you last night.

18. She _had been_ such a nice girl before she died.

19. Peter _has gone_ to America many times.

20. He _has been working_ hard since last year. He _hopes_ to

succeed in the college entrance examination this time.

【練習十八】

1. I will go to church tomorrow.
2. He will meet me next Monday.
3. He will clean this room tomorrow.
4. I will go to Taipei after dinner tomorrow.
5. I will call you tomorrow night after I go home.
6. I will major in law after I graduate.
7. I will watch TV tomorrow after you leave.
8. I will go to Tainan tomorrow.
9. I will write a letter to you tonight.
10. I will wait for my brother tonight.

【練習十九】

1. I _am going to be_ in America next year after I _graduate_.
2. I _will explain_ this to you tonight after I _read_ the report.
3. I _will see_ you tonight.
4. As soon as you _come_ to see me, I _will give_ you my book.
5. When you _arrive_ in New York tomorrow, Tom _will be_ in the airport to meet you.
6. I _will go_ to church after the rain stops.
7. I _will watch_ the new TV program after you _leave_.
8. When you _get_ here tomorrow, everyone _will be waiting_ for

you.

9. I __will get__ a job as soon as I get out of college.

10. He __will have__ dinner very late tomorrow.

11. I __will quit__ my present job, after I __find__ a better one.

【練習二十】

1. I __will be watching__ the baseball game tomorrow night.

2. He __will have finished__ the report when you arrive at his home.

3. I __will have washed__ my car tonight when my mother comes.

4. They __will be playing__ their violins when the clock strikes twelve.

5. He __will have completed__ writing this program before ten o'clock tonight.

6. He __will have been__ the president for three years next May.

7. I __will have repaired__ my car when you come tonight.

8. I __will have read__ this report before six o'clock tomorrow evening.

9. People __will be dancing__ in the streets if Mr. Robertson is elected President.

10. I __will have driven__ four hundred miles tomorrow.

【練習二十一】

1. Perterson was born in 1965. He liked music when he was a

child. Since 1975, he has been learning to play the violin. Now, he is a very good violinist.

2. I will be watching TV at home when my elder brother visits me tomorrow. I like to watch programs about hospitals.

3. I liked to play basketball when I was a child.　Now, I don't because I had a car accident.

4. I am calling my mother, who is eighty-eight years old and has lived in Taipei for sixty years.

5. I had been to England before I went to America. When I was in England, I met a beautiful girl and she has become my wife.

【練習二十二】

1. I　_am watching_　TV now. I　_watch_　TV every day.

2. He　_had had_　a big dinner before we arrived last night. It <u>was</u> a good meal. He seldom　_ate_　so much.

3. He　_has been working_　on this novel for a very long time. By the time he _finishes_　it, he _will have written_ six novels.

4. I　_have been_ to America several times. I　_will go_ to America again next year.

5. I　_lived_　in Taipei when I was a child. When I was six years old, I　_moved_　to Taiwan and　_have lived_　there ever since.

6. It　_is_　my birthday tomorrow. Yet I　_have_　a test the day after tomorrow. So I　_will study_　in the library tomorrow

night.

7. He had been a strong kid before he became an athlete in college. Now although he is seventy years old, he is still quite healthy.

8. He takes a bath every morning. Today, since he got up very late, he went to school directly without taking a bath.

【練習二十三】

1. I didn't see your brother last night.

2. I don't like apples.

3. She is not a beautiful girl.

4. They cannot play violin very well.

5. Mr. Chang must not answer the following questions.

   Mr. Chang does not have to answer the following questions.

6. He didn't go to see his brother last night.

7. He couldn't sing many songs.

8. He will not buy this car.

9. It didn't rain heavily last night.

10. I have not lived here for three years.

11. He doesn't have to see his mother.

12. He didn't have to stay here yesterday.

【練習二十四】

1. I have __no__ money.

2. A selfish person does __not__ have any friends.

3. __No__ man is entirely alone.

4. __No__ one is living here. We can __not__ get into this house.

5. __Not__ a single person loves me.

6. __No__ one loves me.

7. The person whom I saw did __not__ come.

8. I did __not__ go to work yesterday.

9. I had __no__ work to do yesterday.

10. I can __not__ find any one in this hall.

11. I have __neve r__ gone to America.

12. He has __never__ written to me.

【練習二十五】

1. Do you like him?

2. Is he an American?

3. Did you go to church yesterday?

4. Has he been to Japan?

5. Do you want to go to Taipei?

6. Doesn't he like sports?

7. Haven't you been to Japan?

8. Does he have a sister?

9. Are they students?

10. Did your brother see my father yesterday?

【練習二十六】

1. Where did you buy this book?

2. When did he go to America?

3. What is his father's name?

4. Whose book is this?

5. Where are you from?

6. Which book do you want?

7. Who is this kid?

8. Whom does he like most?

9. What is his name?

10. Where did you go yesterday?

11. Whose dog is this?

【練習二十七】

1. _Where_ did you go last night?

2. _Which_ book do you like?

3. _Who_ is your brother?

4. _What_ is his name?

5. _Who_ wrote this letter?

6. _Whom_ did you give this book to?

7. _Who_ gave you this book?

8. _Whose_ car is this?

9. _Whose_ dog is this?

10. _Which_ movie did you see?

11. _Who_ can speak English?

12. _Whom_ did you speak to?

13. _What_ kind of car is this?

14. _Which_ fruit do you like most?

15. _Who_ does not swim?

【練習二十八】

1. That movie was seen by him last night.

2. That letter was written to me by him.

3. Those English classes are taught by him.

4. You are loved by God.

5. Two houses were bought by them.

6. This room was painted by me.

7. Those roses are grown by him.

8. His students are helped by him.

9. The house was sold by me.

10. This car was bought by my uncle.

【練習二十九】

1. I saw the policeman.

2. I wrote those two books.

3. My teacher corrected these sentences.

4. A car hit him.

5. I locked his door.

6. My father built his house.

7. My father gave his boat to me.

8. People here rarely see this bird.

People rarely see this bird here.

9. Everyone likes him.

10. Their friends gave them ten dollars.

11. He took this picture.

12. The young men drank too much wine.

13. Mr. Wang taught me.

14. His father helped him.

15. That waiter served them.

16. My mother prepared his food.

17. My sister made his toy.

18. Jim returned the book to me.

19. My brother wrote that song.

20. He invited me to a party.

【練習三十】

1. Three novels have been written by him.

2. That letter will be written by him.

3. These songs will be sung by them tomorrow.

4. The speech will be given by him.

5. The house is being painted by them.

6. Three books have been given to him by me.

7. This job can be done by me.

8. That story had been told to me by him before we went there.

9. The students should be helped by the teachers.

10. The report is being written by him now.

11. This book must be read by the students.

12. This letter has to be given to my mother by me tonight.

13. The law ought to be obeyed by all citizens.

14. All of the cakes have been eaten by him.

15. Pictures were being taken by the reporters when the storm started.

16. The work had been finished by him before five o'clock last night.

17. That letter will be written by Peter.

18. My letter has been received by John.

19. The movie *Gone with the Wind* was seen by millions of people

20. That theorem has been proved by him.

【練習三十一】

1. Joseph has written two books.

2. Many students are choosing football.

3. His father should give him that lecture.

4. He will write that report.

5. The King has received the letter.

6. Everyone should see this movie.

7. Every student ought to read this book.

8. I am helping them.

9. All of us are going to see the movie.

10. Kids can eat this cake.

【練習三十二】

1. Apples are not grown by the farmers here.

2. I was not met by him last night.

3. That letter has not been written by me.

4. That movie is not going to be seen by John.

5. That movie was not filmed by me.

6. English is not spoken by him.

7. English will not be spoken by him.

8. That cake should not be eaten by you.

9. That kind of fish is not eaten by my mother.

10. That report has not been written by John.

【練習三十三】

1. He did not write the book.

2. You are not going to help me.

3. John has not received that book.

4. College students do not like that song.

5. Mary does not love John.

6. My students will not meet me tomorrow.

7. Vegetarians do not eat meat.

8. I did not open the door.

9. I did not pay those ten dollars.

10. I did not buy the car.

【練習三十四】

1. Is a book being written by him?

2. Was that book written by him?

3. Was that letter signed by you?

4. Where was that movie seen by you?

5. When was that movie seen by you?

6. Has that job been finished by him?

7. Were you given the gift by mother?

8. Were you visited by your mother last night?

9. Are roses grown by them?

10. Is English spoken by them?

11. Was that game of tennis won by you?

12. Will English be taught by you?

【練習三十五】

1. Did you eat the cake?

2. Do all of us like him?

3. Does everyone in Japan love that kind of music?

4. Do old people eat fish?

5. Do most women love roses?

6. Did you call him?

7. Does John play soccer?

8. When did Mozart write this music?

9. When did you see him?

10. Did you see them last night?

【練習三十六】

1. I <u>sent</u> two letters yesterday. <u>Did</u> you <u>receive</u> them? Every letter <u>was written</u> by me. Please <u>write</u> back to me soon.

2. I <u>was invited</u> to a dancing party last week. The music <u>was</u> so noisy. I <u>left</u> the party as early as I <u>could</u>.

3. Did you <u>write</u> that report? Yes, it <u>was written</u> by me.

4. He <u>did not like</u> music when he was a child. After he <u>got</u> into college, he <u>was taught</u> by a good music professor. Now, he <u>enjoys</u> music very much and <u>listens</u> to classical music every morning.

5. I <u>bought</u> a red car yesterday. It <u>was made</u> in Japan. It will <u>be delivered</u> to me tomorrow.

6. I _did not go_ to school yesterday because my bicycle was stolen .

I _bought_ a new bike yesterday.

7. Where _did_ (do) you go last night? I _could_ (can) not find_ (find) you. You _were seen_ (see) by no one.

8. A: Does_ he _smoke ?

B: No, he _does not_. Smoking has never _been tried_ by him.

9. Was the book _written_ by him?

10. I _bought_ three books lately. One _was written_ by Graham Greene.

I _finished_ reading it. There _are_ many interesting stories in it.

【練習三十七】

1. This is a book which _was written_ by Dickens.

2. _Is_ the music enjoyed by those elderly people?

3. When _were_ you visited by your father yesterday?

4. This book _was_ written by John.

5. He _was_ invited to come to my home by my father yesterday.

6. This house _was_ built in 1913.

7. This letter _was_ written by him.

8. This letter has never __been__ finished.

9. __Were__ you given a book?

10. I have never __been__ called by my father. I always call him first.

【練習三十八】

1. Playing tennis is fun.

2. I hate swimming.

3. Stop talking about me.

4. In addition to reading interesting books, you should also watch TV from time to time.

5. I am not interested in swimming.

6. He talks about going to America.

7. I believe in doing exercise every day.

8. The cost of transferring a student to another school is very high.

9. Please forgive me for making this mistake.

10. Swimming keeps me from getting cold.

【練習三十九】

1. Please forgive me __for__ __being__ so late.

2. In addition __to__ __studying__ ,you should also have some exercise every day.

3. We talked __about__ __building__ a house next year.

4. Thank you _for_ _helping_ me.

5. He is excited _about_ _traveling_ to Japan.

6. I am looking forward _to_ _meeting_ you.

7. He insists _on_ _talking_ to me personally.

8. I believe _in_ _exercising_ every day.

9. Did you participate _in_ that _swimming_ match.

10. He was not used _to_ _listening_ to classical music.

11. My mother objected _to_ _visiting_ my aunt tomorrow.

12. I am not accustomed _to_ _going_ to bed so late.

13. I am interested _in_ _swimming_.

14. Are you responsible _for_ _writing_ this report?

15. He is excited _about_ _seeing_ me tomorrow.

16. He is looking forward _to_ _seeing_ that movie.

17. I am not used _to_ _hearing_ that kind of noise.

18. You should take advantage _of_ _having_ such a good family.

19. He is in charge _of_ _sending_ students to other schools.

【練習四十】

1. I do not like dancing.

2. Are you interested in swimming?

3. Playing basketball is interesting.

4. We talked about teaching English yesterday.

5. I am not used to smoking.

6. I object to crying in public.

7. In addition to swimming, he should play baseball.

8. He is capable of running one kilometer every day.

9. He is in charge of finding a good place.

10.　I am accustomed to getting up early.

【練習四十一】

1. I enjoy __listening__ to rock and roll music.

2. I asked him __to go__ away.

3. He was asked __to leave__.

4. I suggest __having__ some fun.

5. He seems __to be__ a kind person.

6. You appear __to be__ (be) quite tired.

7. I told him __to have__ a cup of wine.

8. I invited him __to come__ over.

9. Everyone of you is required __to work__ hard.

10. Do you like __swimming__?

11. I ordered him __to read__ my book.

12. I was expected __to write__ a letter to you.

13. He asked me __to read__ this letter to him.

14. Please keep __talking__ (talk) to me.

15. Stop __driving__ so fast. It is dangerous to drive too fast.

16. I hate __smoking__.

17. __Passing__ (pass) the test is important.

18. <u>Working</u> hard is the key to success.

19. My wife asked me to <u>bring</u> some flowers home.

20. He avoided <u>telling</u> lies.

【練習四十二】

1. I invited him to come to my house.

2. I teach him swimming.

3. To be loved makes people happy.

4. I hate smoking.

5. We should avoid smoking.

6. Stop smoking .

7. Everyone expects him to write a good book.

8. I required him to study English every day.

【練習四十三】

1. He lets his son drive his car.

2. He made me feel happy.

3. I made my friend discuss his problem with me.

4. I had my son get up early every morning.

5. I helped my father paint his house.

6. I had my brother carry this heavy luggage for me.

7. I had Mary marry me.

8. This song makes everyone cry.

9. I helped Nancy work hard.

10. He made us believe him.

11. I saw him play.

12. I heard Mary sing several songs.

13. I watched her swim.

14. I saw the birds fly away.

【練習四十四】

1. This is an interesting storybook.

2. The class is very boring.

3. Look at that singing bird.

4. That smiling man is my brother.

5. People living in the country are usually very healthy.

6. I do not know that boy riding a bicycle.

7. The kid eating ice cream is my son.

8. The student asking questions is pretty clever.

9. Have you met the boy playing basketball?

10. That dying patient is my teacher.

【練習四十五】

1. I am interested in music.

2. The movie seen by everyone was produced in Hollywood.

3. He came from a broken family.

4. The law of the country has broken down.

5. I am excited about this news.

6. We should help that depressed student.

7. Three people got killed in this traffic accident.

8. This is a confused student.

9. He is an interesting person.

【練習四十六】

1. He is totally _confused_.

2. I am _interested_ in seeing that movie.

3. This movie is really _exciting_.

4. That is a _broken_ promise.

5. He has a _broken_ arm.

6. Their marriage was _broken_ up.

7. Justice is still not a _realized_ dream.

8. He is a _depressed_ person.

9. The bicycle _ridden_ by the young kid is mine.

10. I do not like to see any person _injured_.

11. I was very much _surprised_ to hear that news.

12. His statements are _encouraging_.

13. The man _talking_ about Hitler is a professor.

14. The man _piloting_ the airplane is quite young.

15. The company _managed_ by Mr. Lee is getting better and better.

16. Poor John now has a _broken_ heart.

17. There are boys and girls _dancing_ in the garden.

18. The _stolen_ jacket has been found.

19. The boy _laughing_ there is not my son.

20. He has a _smiling_ face.

21. This is indeed very _exciting_.

22. This song, _heard_ by almost everyone, was written by me.

23. I don't like the song _written_ by the Beatles.

24. She is a _caring_ woman.

【練習四十七】

1. We all have the duty to pay taxes.

2. We have the right to remain silent.

3. He has the talent to swim.

4. I have no money left to spend.

5. I have no place to go.

6. He is too tired to drive.

7. I am glad to see you.

8. He is smart enough to get into college.

9. My job is to teach kids English.

10. I was surprised to see you.

11. We have lots of things to talk about.

12. He has no friends to talk to.

【練習四十八】

1. I do not know who you are.

2. Please tell me whether you are an American or not.

3. I do not remember whether you drink coffee or not.

4. Please ask your sister if she went to Japan last year.

5. Do you know who he is?

6. Where he is from remains a puzzle.

7. I want to find out whether his brother can swim or not.

8. I know why he is so sad.

9. Do you know when Mary will come?

10. Do you know what happened?

11. I know why the sky is blue.

12. Please tell me where you worked last year.

13. Do you know what he is talking about?

14. I do not understand what his problem is.

【練習四十九】

1. Please tell me why he is so sad.

2. I do not know where she is from.

3. Please tell me how many people there are in this house.

4. Let me know how old you are.

5. Whether he is Japanese or not is a mystery.

6. Do you know who the president of the United States is?

7. May I ask you which kind of coffee you like?

8. I can not remember how old I am.

9. What he is talking about is unclear to me.

10. Do you know why he is coming?

【練習五十】

1. I don't know __which__ book you bought.

2. Do you know __where__ he is from?

3. Please ask him __whether__ he drinks tea or not.

4. __What__ he is thinking about is well known to all of us.

5. Let me guess __how__ old you are.

6. May I ask __why__ you are so sad?

7. I don't know __who__ he is.

8. Do you know __whose__ house this is?

9. This is not __what__ I want.

10. I don't care __who__ you are.

【練習五十一】

1. I told you that you must leave.

2. I am glad that you are here now.

3. That he is an American is unknown to us.

4. Can you imagine that he is Chinese?

5. Do you think that he is Chinese?

6. That Hitler was defeated in the Second World War is an important event in the history of mankind.

7. I do not think that he is a bad student.

8. I am surprised to know that she is from Japan.

9. It is hard to imagine that he does not have a high school diploma.

10. Do you believe that he is innocent?

11. I demand that my students work hard.

12. That the sun rises in the east is a fact.

【練習五十二】

1. I do not believe that he is my brother.

2. I advised him that he should go to America.

3. Do you believe that the earth is round?

4. I told him that he must read this book.

5. I forgot that you are a kid.

6. Can you believe that I can speak English?

7. That he did not show up makes me angry.

8. I think that he is a good man.

9. Do not forget that there are a lot of poor people in the world.

10. I know that he teaches English.

11. I never knew that he is so smart.

12. I know that he can not come over.

13. I hope that he can come.

14. Can you believe that he grew up in Taiwan?

15. I cannot decide whether he should go to college or not.

16. You told me that he went to America last year.

17. This teacher did not know that my father is also a teacher.

18. I'd like to ask him whether he will come to my house tomorrow.

19. Do you know whether this train goes to Taipei or not?

20. Please tell me whether you can speak English or not.

【練習五十三】

1. I saw that kid who was driving fast.

2. We are discussing those students who have problems.

3. Those who swim everyday must be very strong.

4. The person who took/drove me to the Railway Station is my student.

5. The girl whom you met is my sister.

6. I like the poem which you wrote.

7. The professor whom you were talking about is my elder brother.

8. The music that you heard is R & B.

9. I like those books which have pictures in them.

10. I don't know in which city Lincoln was born.

11. I like the CD that you gave me very much.

12. The movie that I saw last night was very boring.

【練習五十四】

1. I saw the man __whom__ you talked about.

2. He is not the man __whom__ we met.

3. Those __who__ cry very often are usually not liked.

4. I like to talk to people __who__ are friendly.

5. I enjoy reading the book __which__ you gave to me.

6. Do you know the person __whom__ everyone knows?

7. Peter is a good singer __who__ practices singing every day.

8. Do you know the Peter __whom__ we talked about?

9. Did you see the person __whom__ I spoke to?

10. I have seen the person __whom__ we talked about.

【練習五十五】

1. He is the man __who__ is very good at English.

2. I don't know the person __whom__ you talked to.

3. This is not the house __where__ the president lives.

4. I do not like anyone __who__ cries frequently.

5. Did you read the book, __which__ you bought last month?

6. Do you know the year __when__ the Second World War ended?

7. Do you know that student __whom__ I taught?

8. I have no idea about the person __whom__ you are talking about.

9. Do you know __whom__ he is talking about?

10. Do you know __whose__ dress it is?

【練習五十六】

1. He is a good student.

2. He is the student whom every teacher likes.

3. I want to be the president.

4. This is the President.

5. Please open a window.

6. The President of the Republic of China will visit the U. S. A. next year.

7. I want to be a good engineer.

8. He is the teacher whom we often talk about.

9. Java is a new computer language.

10. I have a dog.

11. He is the professor who got a/the big award.

12. Where is the train station?

13. Please tell me the address of the post office.

14. Is there a post office here?

15. The sun rises in the east.

16. The universe is very large.

17. Why can't we see the moon in the day time?

18. How old is the President?

【練習五十七】

1. He is __the__ student who went to see you.

2. There is _a_ river in this area.

3. I don't want to be _a_ teacher.

4. He wants to become _a_ doctor.

5. No one wants to be _a_ beggar.

6. Please open _the_ door which opens to the hall.

7. UNIX is _a_ computer operating system.

8. WINDOWS is _the_ only operating system invested in by Microsoft.

9. I have _a_ dog and two cats.

10. Is she _the_ teacher whom we talked about yesterday?

11. _The_ earth is not flat.

12. Is there _a_ hotel around here?

13. Where is _the_ train station.

14. I really like _the_ library.

15. Please give me _a_ glass of water.

16. _The_ wind is getting stronger and stronger.

17. He is _a_ friend of mine.

18. It is hard for _the_ poor to go to college.

19. He is _the_ swimmer who swam across the English Channel.

20. _The_ weather is getting colder and colder.

21. This is _the_ book which I bought yesterday.

22. I don't want to be _a_ professor.

23. I am going to take _a_ vacation next month.

24. John will become _a_ basketball player.

25. I ride _a_ bicycle to work every morning.

【練習五十八】

1. He is _an_ English Professor.

2. This is _an_ easy job.

3. He is just _an_ ordinary person.

4. _A_ friend in need is _a_ friend indeed.

5. Give me _a_ hint.

6. I have _an_ American friend.

7. I will become _an_ engineer.

8. Is he _an_ honest boy?

9. _An_ hour later, he went away.

10. Where is _the_ university library?

11. Is there _a_ university library here?

【練習五十九】

1. Girls are usually good at learning languages.

2. Dogs always chase cats.

3. I have not had water for two hours.

4. There is no life without pain.

5. Love is the most important thing in one's life.

6. He has wisdom.

7. I am losing patience.

8. This is not the time to cry.

9. The pain due to losing a loved one is hard to endure.

10. The joy of being a father is really great.

11. Being honest is a virtue.

12. We need air to live.

13. I do not drink coffee. I drink tea.

14. We Chinese eat rice every day.

15. The water in this area is very clean.

16. There was a fire in the next street last night.

17. The fire last night killed three kids.

18. The coffee which you are drinking is from South America.

19. Mary is from Canada.

20. China is a large country.

21. The Republic of China was founded in 1911.

22. Where is England?

23. Is Russia in Europe?

24. President Lincoln was a great person.

25. King George was a mad king.

26. The Yellow River is a long river.

27. Have you been to the Gobi Desert?

28. The Manila Bay is very beautiful.

29. It is hard to cross the Atlantic Ocean by a small boat.

30. Can you swim across the English Channel?

31. The United States of America is a large country.

32. The United Nations and the Red Cross often work together.
33. When did the Ottoman Empire end?
34. The British Empire was large before.
35. The Catholic Church is one of the oldest organizations in the world.
36. This cup was made in the Ming Dynasty.
37. The European Renaissance was a very important era for the mankind.
38. We should not go back to the Dark Ages.
39. The Wangs did not invite me to their house.
40. I do not like the Kennedys.
41. The Chinese pay great attention to education.
42. I do not like physics.
43. Are you interested in chemistry?
44. Did you have lunch?
45. Let us have dinner together.
46. I always have breakfast with my family.
47. I had a big dinner last night.
48. The dinner my mother cooked for me was delicious.
49. I go to church every Sunday.
50. He does not like to go to school.
51. Did you see the beautiful church in the next street
52. English is so hard for me.

53. Do you speak English?

54. Do you play tennis?

55. Swimming is good for you.

【練習六十】

1. Boys usually do not like to sit still for long.

2. I would love to have _a_ cup of coffee.

3. There is love between us.

4. Can you feel _the_ love of your mother?

5. _The_ joy of having a new baby is really great.

6. We can not live without love.

7. I have not drunk wine for a long time.

8. Do you have _the_ wisdom to distinguish bad persons from good ones?

9. This is _a_ good dinner.

10. I did not have dinner.

11. _The_ joy of being _a_ mother is great.

12. _Running_ is _a_ good exercise.

13. _The_ sadness due to the death of his mother really hurts him.

14. We need water to live.

15. We can not live without air.

16. I do not drink coffee.

17. _The_ fire that occurred last night destroyed my house.

18. _The_ coffee which you are drinking is very light.

19. _The_ Republic of China is in Asia.

20. Where is Russia?

21. Is France in Africa?

22. President Kennedy was liked by most Americans before be died.

23. _The_ Amazon River is a long one.

24. Have you ever been to Tokyo?

25. Have you ever been to _the_ Tokyo Bay?

26. There are more than one hundred countries in _the_ United Nations.

27. This is _a_ Ming Dynasty porcelain.

28. _The_ Wangs invited us to a dinner party.

29. I do not like mathematics.

30. Spring is a pleasant season.

31. I had _a_ pleasant evening with my friends.

32. _The_ breakfast which I had this morning was too light for me.

33. It is not easy to study English.

34. I did play basketball yesterday.

35. Swimming is good exercise.

36. There should be _a_ chicken in every pot.

【練習六十一】

1. Dogs can bark.

2. Cats can catch mice.

3. Sometimes, suffering is good.

4. I don't drink tea.

5. The feeling of being loved is very important.

6. Speaking the truth makes one happy.

7. We need love.

8. He is a Chinese.

9. The Chinese love drinking tea.

10. Last night, there was a fire in the city.

11. John is from America.

12. Where is France?

13. I like President Lincoln.

14. The Yellow River is not yellow.

15. The Red Cross is one hundred years old.

16. The Ming Dynasty was an important era.

17. Do you like mathematics?

18. I did not eat breakfast this morning.

19. I have already had lunch.

20. I did not go to church yesterday.

21. I will go to college this fall.

22. Swimming makes me strong.

【練習六十二】

1. smaller

2. slower

3. more intelligent

4. more expensive

5. taller

6. shorter

7. more important

8. cheaper

9. more famous

10. colder

11. faster

12. more careful

13. more colorful

14. longer

15. darker

16. brighter

【練習六十三】

1. cuter

2. wider

3. earlier

4. happier

5. heavier

6. thinner

7. easier

8. hotter

9. wiser

10. larger

11. better

12. worse

13. more

【練習六十四】

1. He is older than I.

2. She is younger than I.

3. This university is larger than that university.

4. He is older than my brother.

5. His house is older than mine.

6. The size of this city is larger than that of San Francisco.

7. She is taller than he.

8. The height of this boy is greater than that of his brother.

9. He is the best student in my class.

10. He is the worse one.

【練習六十五】

1. You are stronger than he.

2. His English is better than mine.

3. He is richer than his brother.

4. He is the richest person in the world.

5. This pen is more expensive than yours.

6. He is the tallest man on earth.

7. The Amazon River is the longest river in the world.

8. He is taller than his father.

9. He is the best student in his class.

10. Among the persons whom I have met, he is the tallest.

【練習六十六】

1. He is _older_ than John.

2. This problem is one of _the most difficult_ problems that I have ever seen.

3. This is one of the _best_ movies that I have ever seen.

4. Do we have a _better_ choice?

5. This place is _hotter_ than San Francisco.

6. He is _more famous_ than his sister.

7. She is getting _worse_ now.

8. He is feeling _better_ now.

9. He has _more_ money than his father.

10. Mary is one of _the most beautiful_ students in her class.

11. He is _happier_ than before.

12. Peter is getting _thinner_.

13. This summer is _hotter_ than last summer.

14. You have a _brighter_ future now.

15. He has __more__ students than I.

16. I feel much __better__ now.

17. He is __more careful__ than you.

18. Time is __more important__ than money.

【練習六十七】

1. Many people like to drink wine.

2. He loves you.

3. He wants to go to school.

4. Do you like swimming?

5. I told him to come back soon.

6. I asked my brother to eat an apple every day.

7. My school classmates like to get together.

8. My government wishes to establish a peaceful society.

9. Tom never works hard.

10. He does not tell the truth.

11. I will not go to the concert.

12. I liked to swim.

13. It is important to go to church every Sunday.

14. I was with my brother when you called.

15. My friends are friendly to me.

16. The governments of Asia have no choice

17. His wish to succeed in many things is not realistic.

18. My wish to visit many countries is finally fulfilled.

19. I am a person who eats an apple every day.

20. He is not a good student.

21. Many people are excited by the news.

22. The future is bright.

23. This was caused by the war.

24. How can we obtain lasting peace?

25. How can we succeed?

26. Good citizens love their country.

27. I never watch TV.

28. He has published many books since 1989.

29. I have lived here since I was ten years old.

30. He was in the university when the war broke out.

31. Many Jewish people were killed during the Second World War.

32. I have been a Catholic since 1939.

33. Many people are leaving that country because of the poverty.

34. He was writing a letter when I visited him yesterday.

35. He was happy when he was informed of the good news.

36. He has written many novels.

37. I have finally finished the letter.

38. He is not loved by anyone.

39. Wine is manufactured here.

40. His effort is well appreciated.

41. I like playing basketball.

42. We should pay attention to writing good English sentences.

43. Instead of playing guitar, he plays violin.
44. This is a losing team.
45. He has a smiling face.
46. Why did he cry so loudly?
47. He does not like his brother.
48. He does not speak English.
49. Among all of your students, whom do you like most?
50. He is loved by everyone.
51. This problem is transformed into another problem.
52. This line is connected to the central office.
53. The books will be mailed to you.
54. He is the man who stole my car.
55. Peter is the boy who runs very fast.
56. I did not know that the war broke out so soon.
57. The boys who study hard will easily succeed.
58. There are a lot of people who use computers now.
59. I will let you drive my new car.
60. He makes everyone laugh.
61. I heard him sing.
62. He is making his son go abroad.
63. I will never let him cheat.
64. His mother makes him get up early in the morning.
65. He is excited about the news.
66. He is not interested in sports.

67. This is not interesting to me.

68. His work is well appreciated by all of us.

69. I am disappointed.

70. President Lee will appear soon.

71. It will never happen.

72. He is the most frustrated person.

73. He is living in poverty.

74. There is no possibility of war.

75. Everyone knows who he is.

76. Do you know why he is so happy?

77. It is hard to explain why John failed.

78. He is the cleverest person on earth.

79. Is he getting bigger?

80. This is the taller building.

專門替中國人寫的英文基本文法(修訂版)

2000年11月初版　　　　　　　　　　　　　　　定價：新臺幣230元
2001年7月初版第八刷
2001年9月二版
2022年11月二版四十五刷
有著作權‧翻印必究
Printed in Taiwan.

著　　　者	李	家	同
		海	柏
責任編輯	許	純	青
校　　對	林	淑	宛
封面設計	吳	惠	菁

出　版　者	聯 經 出 版 事 業 股 份 有 限 公 司	副總編輯	陳	逸	華
地　　　址	新北市汐止區大同路一段369號1樓	總 編 輯	涂	豐	恩
叢書主編電話	(0 2) 8 6 9 2 5 5 8 8 轉 5 3 0 5	總 經 理	陳	芝	宇
台北聯經書房	台 北 市 新 生 南 路 三 段 9 4 號	社　　長	羅	國	俊
電　　　話	(0 2) 2 3 6 2 0 3 0 8	發 行 人	林	載	爵
台中辦事處	(0 4) 2 2 3 1 2 0 2 3				
台中電子信箱	e-mail:linking2@ms42.hinet.net				
郵 政 劃 撥 帳 戶	第 0 1 0 0 5 5 9 - 3 號				
郵 撥 電 話	(0 2) 2 3 6 2 0 3 0 8				
印　刷　者	世 和 印 製 企 業 有 限 公 司				
總　經　銷	聯 合 發 行 股 份 有 限 公 司				
發　行　所	新北市新店區寶橋路235巷6弄6號2F				
電　　　話	(0 2) 2 9 1 7 8 0 2 2				

行政院新聞局出版事業登記證局版臺業字第0130號

本書如有缺頁，破損，倒裝請寄回台北聯經書房更換。　ISBN　978-957-08-2284-7 (平裝)
聯經網址 http://www.linkingbooks.com.tw
電子信箱 e-mail:linking@udngroup.com

國家圖書館出版品預行編目資料

專門替中國人寫的**英文基本文法** /李家同、海柏著 .
二版 . 新北市 . 聯經 . 2001年 . 328面 . 14.8×21公分 .
ISBN　978-957-08-2284-7(平裝)
[2022年11月二版四十五刷]

1.英國語言-文法

805.16　　　　　　　　　　　　　　　90014004